# A Springtime Scandal

A Lord For All Seasons
Book 1

## Nadine Millard

## ARE YOU SIGNED UP FOR DRAGONBLADE'S BLOG?

You'll get the latest news and information on exclusive giveaways, exclusive excerpts, coming releases, sales, free books, cover reveals and more.

Check out our complete list of authors, too!

No spam, no junk. That's a promise!

### Sign Up Here

www.dragonbladepublishing.com

*Dearest Reader;*

*Thank you for your support of a small press. At Dragonblade Publishing, we strive to bring you the highest quality Historical Romance from some of the best authors in the business. Without your support, there is no 'us', so we sincerely hope you adore these stories and find some new favorite authors along the way.*

*Happy Reading!*

*CEO, Dragonblade Publishing*

# Prologue

"MRS. TEMPLEWORTH, I cannot tell you how helpful Elodie has been during our preparations for the ball. Truly, she is grace and kindness itself."

Mrs. Templeworth smiled at Mrs. Bell before her eyes moved to her eldest daughter.

Even now, Elodie was conferring with Reverend Bell about some detail or other.

The reverend's wife was hosting her annual ball at the Assembly Rooms in aid of the local orphans' home, and Elodie was, as usual, giving everything she had to the cause.

Elodie had always been kind.

From the time she was in short skirts, she was the one who'd brought home stray animals, helped Cook in the kitchen, and as her younger siblings came along, acted like a mother hen clucking over her baby chicks.

Sometimes Mrs. Templeworth worried that Elodie was *too* good. She worried that her daughter could be easily taken advantage of. But, in their particular part of Surrey, at least, the people cared for and respected Elodie and didn't abuse her generous nature.

And Mrs. Templeworth didn't think that Elodie would venture far from their little corner of England. Though she had yet to have her Come Out, it was doubtful that Elodie would enjoy a Season. Town wouldn't appeal with the noise, the smells, the bustle, or the crowds.

Hope, Elodie's younger sister, would be enamored of it all. Even Francesca. And Lord only knew what Sophia would be like as a young debutante since she was a veritable hoyden of a child.

A screech from outside the Assembly Rooms rent the air, and Elodie looked up, her deep brown eyes widening in concern.

She rushed to the window, Mrs. Templeworth only seconds behind her.

In the yard, Francesca and Sophia chased each other around, Francesca hitching her skirts and running in a way that Mrs. Templeworth was sure would turn her hair white.

Sophia, at least, was still a girl of twelve. Francesca, at fourteen years old, should know better.

And where was Hope, who should have been watching her younger siblings?

Mrs. Templeworth ran her gaze around the yard until she spotted sixteen-year-old Hope.

Judging from Elodie's gasp of dismay, she, too, had seen Hope leaning against the carriage, batting her eyelashes at a young stablehand.

"Is anything the matter?"

Elodie and Mrs. Templeworth both spun around at the sound of Mrs. Bell's voice.

"No!" Elodie exclaimed, her laugh strained, her cheeks flushed. "No, nothing at all. Um—I think—I think that we ought to be heading home."

She looked desperately at Mrs. Templeworth, who immediately nodded her agreement.

"Yes, plenty to be done to get the girls ready. Hope is so excited about attending her first event," Elodie said weakly.

They bid a swift farewell to Reverend and Mrs. Bell before they hurried outside, Elodie flying ahead of her mother.

Once they were out in the bright spring sunshine, Elodie rushed over to Hope.

She dismissed the stablehand, who walked unsteadily away,

looking a little dazed from his encounter with Hope.

As soon as the yard was clear, Elodie glared at her sister.

"What do you think you are doing?" she hissed.

Hope rolled her chocolate-brown eyes, the exact shade of her sister's.

"Having fun, Elodie," she drawled. "A concept that is alien to you, I know."

Mrs. Templeworth left them to their arguing and hurried to round up the other two.

She wondered if they'd been hasty in letting Miss Simmons, the girls' governess, visit her sister for a week. Fewer hands meant more trouble, after all. At least when it came to the younger Templeworth girls.

"You cannot flirt outrageously with stableboys in full view of the vicar and his wife, Hope. That is not the type of 'fun' young ladies should be partaking of."

"And how would you know?" Hope bit back as Mrs. Templeworth corralled Francesca and Sophia into the carriage. "You wouldn't know what fun was if it jumped up and bit you."

All the way home, the girls bickered.

Francesca sulked about not being allowed to attend the ball that night.

Sophia was squalling because she hadn't been allowed to bring home the snail she'd found in the grass.

And Elodie was still begging Hope to behave herself that evening.

"Hope, our family's reputation is at stake," she said now. "If you get yourself involved in a scandal, *any* sort of scandal, the rest of us will be quite ruined. Don't you understand that?"

The carriage pulled up in front of the large, redbrick house, and the girls tumbled out, only Elodie and Mrs. Templeworth exiting with any sort of decorum.

"Of course I understand, Elodie," Hope sighed while she removed her straw bonnet. "I would never bring any sort of disgrace to the family name. But none of us can be the paragon that you are. And none of us has any wish to be."

Elodie opened her mouth, no doubt to argue, but Hope continued, not letting her sister speak.

"You continue being Miss Perfect, never putting so much as a fingernail wrong. And I'll concentrate on enjoying myself."

Hope swept walked one way, Elodie stomped another, whilst Francesca and Sophia dashed off to the kitchen to coax Cook into parting with some of her famous apple tartlets.

Mrs. Templeworth stood still in the abrupt quiet, relishing the silence, despairing of the ringing in her ears.

She worried about her girls. Despite the best efforts of she and Miss Simmons, the younger three had a wildness about them that she feared was irrepressible.

Elodie would never dishonor the Templeworth name. Elodie was their great hope.

She would conduct herself in a way above reproach, attract a respectable husband, and hopefully set them all down a path of good marriages and good reputations.

If anyone could do it, Elodie could.

# Chapter One

*Two Years Later...*

ELODIE TEMPLEWORTH TRIED her very best to ignore the fact that Hope was standing extremely close to George Foster, the magistrate's son with a bit of a reputation, and that Francesca was drinking a third glass of champagne.

Keeping in mind that she'd been forbidden from drinking *any* champagne at all, three was actually a compromise when it came to Francesca. And Elodie had to remind herself of that, lest she run over there and draw attention to the situation by forcibly removing the flute from Cheska's hand.

She tried to ignore the knot of anxiety in her stomach as she carefully scrutinized the faces of those around her, checking to see if they noticed her sisters' less than decorous behavior.

And, of course, then came the inevitable flare of annoyance at herself for thinking this way.

Elodie couldn't say why she was so obsequious. So desperate for the approval of others. She always had been.

Sometimes she envied her younger sisters their freedom of thought and action.

Hope was flighty and flirtatious, and much as Elodie worried about the disgrace that would befall them all, thus far, there hadn't been a whiff of scandal around her younger sister.

But then, Hope was on the verge of her first Season in London. And whilst people in their village might tolerate Hope's frivolity, London, Elodie knew, was sure to be a different matter entirely.

This would be Elodie's second Season. And she knew in a way her sister didn't, that there were gentlemen in London who would think nothing of destroying a lady's reputation and then leaving her to rot. Not that Elodie had any first-hand experience of such a thing. She'd stayed firmly on the sidelines watching young lady after young lady be taken in by blackguards. Elodie would never allow herself to be in such a situation. But Hope?

At that moment, Hope looked up and caught Elodie's stare. She rolled her eyes and pointedly turned her back, her caramel-colored curls bouncing as she swung away from Elodie's attention.

Deciding that, at least for the moment, Hope was relatively safe, Elodie turned her attention to Francesca.

Lord, was that a fourth glass?

That certainly needed intercepting.

Elodie moved gracefully and unhurriedly to the other side of the Assembly Room, where Cheska was giggling, her cheeks more flushed than usual.

If she hurried, people might be alerted to the situation.

As she went, people called their greetings and congratulations on another successful charity ball.

She'd been helping the reverend for years, not only to organize these events but in the orphanage itself.

And people knew that as time went on, Elodie's involvement became more and more important as the reverend and his wife grew older and less able.

Elodie smiled and gently pried herself from attempts at conversation.

At last, she reached the place where Cheska now stood with a gathering of like-minded revelers.

"Cheska."

The group turned at the sound of her voice, and the gentlemen all bowed deferentially.

She'd known these men all her life, and whilst she knew that most of them were relatively harmless, there were some whom she absolutely didn't want foxed around her little sister.

Elodie could tell by Cheska's expression that she was disappointed at Elodie's appearance, and she tried not to feel stung by that.

Just as she tried not to be too severe upon her sister. This was Cheska's first real event. Just like two years ago at Hope's first ball, Cheska had been giddy with excitement for weeks.

Elodie didn't remember ever feeling particularly giddy in her life, but surely, she had been before her first ball?

"I wasn't doing anything, Elodie," Cheska said mutinously before Elodie spoke even a word.

And Elodie felt hurt all over again.

"I know," she said. "I just—I wondered if—"

Before she could finish what she was going to say, the dance master announced a reel, and Cheska was whisked away in a flurry of white skirts and golden curls. Her hair was a brighter shade than Hope's toffee-colored tresses, but her eyes weren't brown like her older sister's.

"M-miss Templeworth. I believe this set is mine?"

Elodie sent one last concerned look after her sister before turning to smile patiently at Phillip Harrison.

He was a kind and mannerly gentleman farmer, and Elodie was as fond of him as she was of all her childhood acquaintances.

Lately, however, she'd grown concerned that Philip might be forming some sort of attachment to her. And whilst she liked him, she had no romantic interest in him.

Another knot of anxiety twisted her stomach as she took his arm and followed the other dancers.

If her suspicions were right, and Philip ended up proposing, how would she let him down without hurting him?

"You look quite the thing this evening, Miss Templeworth. If I may be so bold."

"Thank you, Mr. Harrison," she said as evenly as she could.

Frankly, she *didn't* want him to be so bold. But she couldn't very well tell him that.

"Are you enjoying the dance?" she asked now, steering the conversation to safe waters.

"Indeed. You have done a wonderful job as usual," he said affably. "Even my cousin thinks so, and he is quite the man about town, so he isn't usually impressed by quiet, country life."

"Oh? I didn't know you had a cousin visiting with you," she said conversationally.

The dance took them away from each other and the opportunity to speak, and Elodie cast her eyes around the occupants of the room whilst she awaited her turn to move down the row of dancers.

She hadn't noticed any new faces earlier, but that signified nothing. The place was packed, and—

Elodie's thoughts came to a screeching halt as her gaze landed upon a stranger. A very tall, very imposing stranger.

And he was staring right at her.

Elodie's eyes widened as she took in the man who stood head and shoulders above everyone around him.

Surely this was Mr. Harrison's cousin. There was no way he'd been in the village before, and she hadn't spotted him.

Why, all around him, ladies were whispering behind their fans and batting their lashes, so he was clearly new to them, too.

And if Hope had known about him, she'd have eaten him alive by now.

But he wasn't looking at Hope or the bevy of ladies around him.

He was looking at her.

Elodie felt her heart pick up speed in the most peculiar way.

She felt as though she couldn't drag her eyes from the man and, as she watched, his lips quirked in the most devilish smile she'd ever seen.

Oh, he was trouble. The very embodiment of it.

Her cheeks grew warm, and she could only imagine that they were flushed now, making obvious the effect the man had on her.

This would simply not to.

The fear of drawing attention to herself broke whatever spell the stranger was weaving, and Elodie was able to turn her nose up piously and turn away.

She promenaded with Philip, danced the rest of the dance, making only polite chitchat, and when the dance ended, allowed him to escort her to where Hope now stood mercifully alone.

"Thank you, Mr. Harrison," she said, hoping he wouldn't linger.

He didn't, and as soon as he'd taken his leave, Hope gripped Elodie's arm.

"Good heavens, Elle, have you seen that man?"

Elodie's stomach flipped, though she couldn't have said why exactly.

"What man?" she asked, pleased that her voice sounded far steadier than her insides felt.

"Um, the *delicious*, tall, brooding stranger in the corner, Elodie," Hope said, rolling her eyes. "Honestly, you wouldn't notice a man standing stark naked in front of you."

"Hope!" Elodie admonished, darting her gaze around to ensure nobody heard her incorrigible sister. "Really. How many times have I told you it is completely inappropriate to speak in such a fashion?"

"Oh, do calm yourself, Elodie. Nobody heard me."

Hope shook her head in her usual nonchalant fashion.

"Nobody is paying attention to *us* because everyone's eyes are on him!"

Elodie could well believe it.

There was something about that man. She had felt it when he'd locked eyes with her. Clearly, everyone else felt it, too.

"Be that as it may, I—"

"Miss Templeworth."

Elodie spun around at the sound of her name being called,

and her heart stuttered all over again.

Mr. Harrison was behind her, and with him, the mystery man.

"May I introduce my cousin, Christian Harrison, Viscount Brentford? Christian, Miss Templeworth and Miss Hope Templeworth."

"An honor, ladies." The tall viscount executed a perfect bow to the sisters.

Elodie desperately scrambled around inside her brain to find her good manners, her sense of propriety, her knowledge of how to behave. But she struggled more than usual.

She stared up at Viscount Brentford, unable to tear her gaze away.

And once again, he was staring right back, his lips quirked in that smile.

From across the room, she hadn't particularly been able to discern his features.

Up close, however, she could drink him in. And that's just what she did.

Her eyes, almost of their own accord, studied every detail of him.

The breadth of his shoulders in his black dinner jacket. The simple ruby pin in his snowy white cravat. The charcoal waistcoat was understated and not at all gaudy like some worn by men who considered themselves dandies.

His hair was a deep walnut color, and his eyes—his eyes were a bright, piercing blue.

When her gaze finally returned to meet them, she felt as though he might be able to see into her soul.

Elodie had never been prone to dramatics. That particular trait was all Sophia's. Yet her reaction to this man whom she'd never met before felt intense and strange and even a little frightening.

Elodie was so entranced that she failed to notice the silence growing awkward, and it was only when Hope subtly nudged her side, that she realized that she hadn't responded.

Cheeks flaming, Elodie dropped a swift curtsey to the gentleman.

"We are so glad you could attend our humble dance, my lord," she said. "I do hope you're enjoying your time in Halton."

"In truth, I have found the slower pace of life difficult to get used to, Miss Templeworth. Though I admit, this place is becoming more interesting by the second."

Elodie couldn't have said why his words caused her heart to stutter, but they did, and her blasted cheeks felt hotter, still.

"I'm sure you could find plenty to interest you, my lord, if you look hard enough."

Hope's voice oozed seduction, and Elodie had a sudden, mad desire to put her hand over her sister's mouth.

She knew how it would go.

Hope would say outrageous things, and the viscount would be infatuated by her in seconds. It was always the way. Hope's golden-haired, doe-eyed beauty was incomparable. Add to it her vivacity and flirtatiousness, and there wasn't a man alive who could resist her.

Elodie dropped her gaze, studying her white satin slippers while she tried not to feel envious.

She'd never been jealous of any of her sisters before, and she didn't particularly enjoy the feeling.

"I think I might have done just that, Miss Templeworth," the viscount's deep, smooth voice interrupted her thoughts, and Elodie couldn't help but look up at him again.

A riot of butterflies burst inside of her. She blinked, full sure that she looked like an owl staring wide-eyed at him.

"Miss Templeworth, would you do me the honor of dancing the next with me?" he asked. "Unless, of course, you are already engaged for it?"

She was engaged for it.

She was to dance with Mr—er—Mr—

She couldn't even remember who!

"She is not engaged, my lord."

Elodie managed to turn a frown of confusion on Hope, who looked innocently back.

"Off you go with the viscount, Elodie," Hope grinned.

She couldn't, of course. She didn't know the man, and he hadn't even been introduced to Mama yet. Elodie would never do something so bold as to dance with a complete stranger.

The strains of a cotillion sounded, the dance master called out the next, and Lord Brentford held out a hand.

*You mustn't, Elodie,* she told herself firmly.

Yet, her hand seemed to have a mind of its own, just as her eyes had earlier.

For without truly knowing why, she placed her hand into the viscount's and allowed him to lead her away.

# Chapter Two

CHRISTIAN WATCHED MISS Elodie Templeworth's expression closely as they stood facing each other, waiting for the dancing to start.

He was a base enough creature to admit that dancing wasn't exactly what he'd like to be doing with the stunning brunette, but dance, he would.

He'd been watching her from the second he'd arrived this evening, and though they'd spoken only a handful of words to each other, he had her figured out.

She was goodness personified.

He knew from the way she conducted herself, from the way she scowled constantly at the two blondes with whom she'd arrived—one of them, an outrageous flirt as he'd just witnessed, the other, a tearaway if her champagne guzzling and raucous laughter was anything to go by.

Miss Elodie had only drunk lemonade.

The dance began, and Christian bowed to his partner, oddly entranced by the flush of pink upon her cheeks.

He wasn't normally attracted to perfect little misses. Too much hard work and not enough payout, in his vast experience. But this one intrigued him.

Christian hadn't meant to stay in this sleepy hamlet for longer than he absolutely had to.

He'd just returned from a trip to the Americas, where he had invested money in various business prospects and had decided to visit his father's younger brother and his family upon his return to England.

Since Christian's father had passed away, and Christian had taken over the viscountcy, he'd come to learn how much his uncle relied on the viscountcy's coffers for finances.

Though his uncle had purchased a vast amount of farmland, he hadn't managed it very well.

When Christian had come to look into the matter, he'd discovered his uncle infirm and his cousin Philip running things.

Philip, as it turned out, was very different from his father. He worked hard and took pride in the family's farms. He had also been unaware of the stipend that Christian's father, and now Christian himself, provided.

Christian had come with the vague intention of ending the agreement, figuring that the land should be paying for itself.

But after he'd met his cousins, his aunt, and even his uncle, he'd found himself unwilling to cut them off.

He had no doubt that Philip would turn a tidy profit on the farms given the time to do so, and truthfully, he liked his cousins, both Philip and his younger sister, and had no desire to hurt them financially or otherwise.

Besides, it wasn't as though he couldn't afford it. Especially after his success in the Americas.

He'd been honest with Philip, told him that he didn't mind the money but that he would rather it be invested in more up-to-date farming practices.

Philip had a passion for farming and the knowledge to make the holding a success, and Christian was, after all, a risk-taker. In business as well as in his personal life.

The cousins had come to an agreement that suited them both, and when Philip had asked Christian to stay on a day or two and attend this little country dance, his newfound affection for his earnest cousin had led him to agree.

When he'd walked in the door, he'd assumed that he'd spend

a few hours being a little bored but was happy to do it for his cousins and aunt, who took great pleasure in showing off a viscount for a nephew.

And then, the Misses Templeworth had arrived.

Philip had been talking of the family since they'd set out for the Assembly Rooms. And for days before, truth be told.

The eldest, he'd said, was a quiet, modest girl who spent her life helping those less fortunate.

Christian had almost fallen asleep listening to Philip's description of the chit. That much goodness came hand in hand with dullness, no doubt about it.

The younger two sounded much more fun.

The youngest, Philip had explained though Christian hadn't asked, was not yet old enough to be out at events, though it wouldn't be too much longer. That one, Philip had said a bit piously to Christian's mind, was going to be more trouble than the other three put together.

But Miss Elodie, the eldest, was by all accounts a veritable paragon.

Christian had felt a fleeting curiosity to see these much talked about Templeworths. Especially the middle ones. Nothing would make the time pass in this quiet village more than a flirtation with a fun-loving country girl.

But nothing could have prepared him for what he'd felt when they'd arrived.

Philip had suddenly stood taller, pulling his straining waistcoat down over his stomach and puffing out his chest.

Christian had spared his cousin a brief grin before looking to see the source of his sudden attention to detail.

And that had been that.

The blondes, he'd guessed, were the younger two, given that one of them was immediately surrounded by an assortment of gentlemen, and the other had flitted toward the refreshments.

But Christian had barely noticed, for he was riveted by the paragon.

It was a testament to Philip's decency, Christian supposed, that the man had spent so long listing the strengths of Miss Templeworth's stalwart and virtuous character and hadn't once mentioned how beautiful she was.

Christian was sure he'd never seen anyone quite so lovely before in his life.

And he'd seen a lot of women.

He'd watched, unable to help himself, as she'd bustled around the place fixing decorations, ensuring the elderly patrons were taken care of, plucking glasses of champagne from one sister, and male hands from the other.

All the while, she'd kept a serene countenance, never once looking less than perfectly poised, perfectly refined.

Though her white gown was demure and ladylike, it didn't hide the graceful curve of her neck or the gentle sway of her hips. If anything, it made her all the more tantalizing to him.

He'd kept his distance while Philip had sought a dance. He'd kept his distance while she'd spoken with first one sister, then the other.

But when she'd caught his gaze during her dance with Philip, Christian had known he wouldn't keep his distance any longer.

Those eyes, the same color as her dark, chestnut hair, had stared at him, beckoning him. And when she'd blushed, a becoming pink stain coloring her cheeks, he'd decided that he would speak to her tonight, dance with her tonight. See if she could possibly be as charming as she appeared.

Christian had sensed Philip's tension when he'd asked Elodie Templeworth to dance, and he suspected that his cousin was more enamored of the lady than he'd even let on.

That should have given Christian pause. And it did, in some respects.

He was London bound, wanting to arrive before the Season so that he could see his men of business and get everything in order before Parliament started.

He had a longstanding arrangement with a mistress there,

one that suited him and his disinterest in marrying.

And he traveled a lot, always had done.

Quiet country dances and the ladies that went with them had never interested him. This was Philip's domain.

But none of that had been quite enough to stop him from wanting to dance with Elodie Templeworth.

And now he was facing her, seeing her face clearly and realizing she was even more beautiful than he'd first imagined.

"You dance very well, Miss Templeworth," he spoke as soon as the steps in the dance brought them close enough to afford the opportunity.

She darted her eyes up to his and blinked rapidly, as though his words were bringing her round from something. He wondered where her mind was.

"Thank you, my lord," she said simply, demurely, with no trace of emotion.

Christian felt a twinge of disappointment.

It might be that Elodie Templeworth was captivatingly lovely. But if she had the personality of a broom, he wouldn't be remotely interested.

Contrary to his past behaviors and his well-earned reputation, Christian was at a point where he was interested in more than just a pretty face. Not for long, mind. But still. He'd rather not be bored to tears by the company he kept.

"Are you enjoying yourself?" he tried again.

"I am, my lord," she answered, still in that same, polite monotone.

His questions weren't exactly riveting, he knew. But he heard enough "yes, my lords" and "no, my lords" as it was. He didn't want to hear them from her.

Perhaps it was just as well, he reasoned as the dance drew to a close.

If Philip was indeed taken with the lady, Christian didn't want to step on his cousin's toes.

The dance ended, and Christian stepped forward to offer Miss

Templeworth his arm, ignoring the bizarre pang of dissatisfaction he felt.

He looked down at her, perhaps to enjoy the view before he left, and was shocked by the expression on her face.

Gone was the modest, decorous, frankly boring expression. Instead, she looked fierce—her eyes flashing, her lips pursed in a scowl that should've made her less attractive but didn't.

"I'll murder her."

Christian felt the flame of interest flicker to life once more, and he moved his gaze to see who was on the receiving end of the sudden death threat.

*Ah.*

*The youngest one.*

He'd seen her earlier, gulping back champagne.

Now it seemed she was starting to feel the effects.

She staggered out of the room, banging off the doorframe on her way.

"Miss Templeworth, I—"

"My lord."

Christian came to a stop as Miss Templeworth interrupted him, turning to face him.

"Thank you for the dance. If you'll excuse me?"

It sounded polite enough, but Christian felt well and truly dismissed. And the truth was, he wasn't used to being dismissed by anyone, let alone the fairer sex.

He watched as she hurried, albeit gracefully, to the other side of the room, leaving him abandoned in the middle of the dancers. And his interest was piqued again.

From the corner of his eye, he saw Philip frowning in his direction.

Miss Templeworth dashed off after her sister.

He should just let her go, of course. He didn't know her, and he was leaving. He should return to Philip and put the man's mind at rest.

Christian hesitated a moment then, wondering at his own sanity, went after her.

# Chapter Three

ELODIE'S HEART RACED as she dashed out of the Assembly Rooms. She would like to think it was due to concern for her younger sister. But she had to be honest with herself, at least.

Her heart was thumping because she'd just danced with Lord Brentford.

Though she was full sure that she'd managed to come across to the man as nothing more than a complete dolt, it didn't change that *frisson* of awareness she'd felt every time his hand touched hers, every time his blue gaze had met with her own.

She'd seen his eyes glaze over with boredom when she'd met his attempts at conversation with her simpering, vacuous responses. But he made her nervous in a way she'd never experienced before, and quite frankly, her brain hadn't been working correctly around him.

Anyway, she didn't have time to worry about the handsome viscount or the fact that he must think her an imbecile now.

Not when she had a rogue sister to track down.

Elodie felt a twinge of irritation that it was she out here in the cold searching for her sister, whilst Mama sat comfortably upstairs with her cronies.

But that had long since been the way of things, and there was little sense in worrying about it now.

She'd never minded before, in any case.

Perhaps it would have been nice to spend a bit longer with

the viscount, but that was neither here nor there.

He would be leaving Halton soon, she was sure. And one country dance would signify nothing to the man.

Elodie searched the empty courtyard to no avail. There was no sign of her sister.

Just where could Cheska have gotten to?

Ironic really, Elodie supposed, that it was Francesca out here and not Hope.

Before she could start to panic, however, a noise caught her attention, and she turned toward the copse of trees that bordered the stables.

A glimpse of white told her that was where her sister was. And the glimpse of a male boot told her Francesca wasn't alone.

"Of all the foolish, idiotic—"

"Do you make a habit of speaking to yourself?"

Elodie gasped as an amused male voice sounded in her ear, and she whipped around to see Lord Brentford smiling down at her.

"What are you doing out here?" she snapped before remembering herself.

She clasped a hand to her mouth.

"I – I mean—"

To her surprise, the viscount, rather than seem insulted, laughed softly.

"I imagine you mean what am I doing out here," he grinned. "Truthfully, I'm not entirely sure. What are *you* doing out here?"

Elodie frowned at his cryptic remark, but she didn't have time to wonder overly much about it.

If she didn't get over to Francesca fast, her entire family would be ruined.

She was going to ring a peal of epic proportions over her sister's foolish head.

"I need to…that is I only wanted to—"

She sighed and stamped her foot in frustration. "Hang it," she said, earning a widening of the viscount's eyes. The truth was there was no way to dress up this particular nasty situation. And the longer she spent there trying to talk her way around it, the more time Cheska had to get into trouble. "My sister is in a spot of bother, and I need to—help. Alone," she said quickly, so she could get rid of him.

With a nod of dismissal, she spun on her heels and dashed away from him.

Reaching the trees, Elodie's stomach sank at the distinctive sound of a giggle, followed by a gasp.

A fury that she frequently felt around her siblings rose up in Elodie, and she marched into the trees, uncaring that twigs and leaves snagged in her hair and gown.

"Francesca!"

Her voice brought an immediate cessation to the activities before her.

Francesca's eyes widened, and she stumbled away from the man whose face had been suspiciously close to her neck.

For one, wild moment, Elodie imagined she and Lord Brentford in a similar position and was appalled by the thrill of excitement that shot through her.

"E-Elodie," Francesca hiccoughed, smiling at her sister. "We were just—"

"I know exactly what you were just doing," she hissed. "And you."

Elodie rounded on the man who turned out to be Albert Truant, the squire's son.

"You should know better, young man," she bit out, even though Albert and she were only months apart in age, and he was, in fact, older than she.

"Come now, Mish Templeworth," Albert slurred, and Elodie realized he was far drunker than she'd thought. Which probably meant that Francesca was, too.

Lord, they'd never live this down.

If anyone knew a gently bred lady was standing in the bushes, completely foxed…

"We're only having a birrofun. Here—why don't you join ush?"

He held out a flask, and even from a distance of two feet, Elodie could smell the potency of whatever was in there.

"Mr. Truant, put that away this instant, and the both of you get inside. And not a word of this to anyone, understand?" she said, well aware that she sounded like a stern governess.

"Oh, for heaven's sake, Elle. When will you learn to loosen up a little? Hope was right about you. Even at a party, you don't know how to relax and have fun."

Elodie sucked in a breath at Francesca's words. They shouldn't hurt. After all, she had prided herself on being the good one, the sensible one. But it did hurt, and the sting of humiliation heated her cheeks.

It didn't help that Albert dratted Truant snickered and snorted like a pig beside Cheska.

"Be that as it may, your behavior is not merely 'enjoying yourself,' Cheska. It's highly likely to ruin you and the rest of us by association. This is your first foray into Society. Do you want it to be your last?"

Cheska blinked at Elodie for a moment.

"No, I don't," she said quietly.

Elodie sighed in relief, thankful that she seemed to have finally gotten through to her sister.

If she managed to get Francesca inside and sobered up away from prying eyes, this whole thing could be smoothed over. They could all go home, and the Templeworth name could live to fight another day.

"Come along, then." She reached out a hand to her foolish younger sister, hoping that whilst she'd been out here putting out one fire, Hope wasn't inside lighting another one.

Francesca took Elodie's hand, and the sisters made to move away.

Before they'd gone more than a couple of steps, however, Mr. Truant reached out and clasped Elodie's shoulder.

"Mish Templeworth, p-please don' be hasty."

He leaned forward, coming alarmingly close to Elodie.

She could smell sweat and something potent on him, not an attractive scent in any way.

"Unhand me, Mr. Truant," she said severely.

He frowned as though confused by her words, then his face cleared, and he grinned stupidly.

"Come now, Elodie. Learn to have a li'l fun."

Elodie felt the beginnings of a headache press against the back of her eyes.

Heaven preserve her from idiotic men in their cups.

Throwing her eyes heavenward to pray for patience, Elodie took a deep breath, then turned to Francesca, who was starting to look a little green.

"Cheska, why don't you run along inside and get some tea?" she spoke as calmly and evenly as she could. "Mr. Truant and I need to have a talk."

Mercifully, Francesca didn't argue, merely nodded her head and hurried off in the direction of the Assembly Rooms.

Even she couldn't get herself into trouble in an empty yard. Or so Elodie hoped.

When they were alone, Elodie turned to face Albert Truant, pulling her arm from his grip.

But he was stronger than he looked—though still woefully unsteady on his feet—and kept hold of her.

"Mr. Truant, please unhand me."

"Elodie—"

"My name is Miss Templeworth," she bit out through gritted teeth. They had grown up in the village together, and ordinarily, Elodie wouldn't have minded a man she'd known since leading-strings using her given name. But his behavior this evening was the outside of enough.

Once more, she attempted to pull her arm away, and once more, his grip remained firm.

"Just what are you about Albert Truant? Get your hand off

me at once."

"Now, now," he slurred, stumbling forward and leaning against her.

Elodie struggled with the weight of him.

"Mr. Truant," she gasped. "Really."

Elodie felt a prickle of fear along her nerves.

She didn't think Albert would hurt her. But then, she'd never really seen him this foxed. And she knew that over-imbibing could change a man. Not enough to turn him into a rapist, perhaps. But certainly enough to have him ignore her obvious attempts to get him off her.

Mr. Truant stumbled again, and Elodie staggered under his weight, her back slamming painfully into a tree.

With one arm still within his grip, she tried in vain to push him away with the other.

"Will you *please*—"

"I suggest you remove yourself from the lady before I do it for you."

Elodie's eyes widened as Lord Brentford stepped forward. Though his voice had been calm and emotionless, there was a fury in his eyes that made Elodie shiver in response.

Albert Truant was not a dangerous man. An idiotic dolt, but not a dangerous one.

Still, she was glad that Lord Brentford had appeared, if only because he looked big enough and strong enough to remove Mr. Truant from her person.

Mr. Truant, for his part, was rather slow on the uptake and was yet to right himself.

"He-he's not attacking me," Elodie gasped under the weight of the great big oaf. "He's just—"

"Cutting off your circulation?" Lord Brentford offered helpfully.

"Quite," she answered, hearing how fed up she sounded even to her own ears.

It was beyond bizarre that she was standing there discussing the situation casually, as though chatting about the weather, with a viscount she'd only met and another man pinning her to a tree.

"Mish Elodie," Mr. Truant finally piped up though he made no effort to move. "You shmell d'licioush."

"Right. That's it."

Before Elodie could wonder at the viscount's words, he leaned forward and plucked Mr. Truant away from her as though the man weighed nothing at all.

Elodie felt an immediate relief as she was able to draw in a proper breath of clean, alcohol-free air.

"Thank you," she gasped, standing away from the tree and shaking out her skirts before looking up. "You—Lord Brentford!"

Lord Brentford had Albert by the scruff, turning the man's skin an alarming shade of puce.

"You would do well to remember your manners in front of a lady," the viscount was still speaking in that oddly calm tone, as though this were an everyday occurrence. "Especially this lady."

Elodie was momentarily distracted from her shock by his words. Especially her? She felt a thrill of *something* but quickly came to her senses.

Rushing forward, she reached an arm out and placed it on the viscount's, ignoring the feel of sinewy muscle evident even through his clothing.

"My lord, really. He meant no harm," she insisted.

Lord Brentford's eyes snapped down to hers, and Elodie was, once again, distracted by the piercing blue depths.

In an instant, however, his gaze was redirected to the floundering Mr. Truant.

"Apologize," he said quietly, sounding more menacing than if he'd shouted.

"M-my apologies, Mish Elodie," Mr. Truant managed to gasp.

The viscount released him, and Mr. Truant stumbled back, pulling at his cravat and gulping in air.

Elodie barely spared the man a nod of forgiveness before he was stumbling off to the Assembly Rooms.

The silence he left behind was deafening, at least to Elodie.

She was embarrassed that Lord Brentford had seen her in such a position, embarrassed that he must have seen Francesca's behavior.

Oh, why hadn't he just gone back inside? Why had he even followed her out here?

"My lord, thank you for your assistance," she began, trying to keep her voice calm and steady. "My sister—she's young. And-and perhaps has over-imbibed a little. But—"

"Why are you the one out here dealing with this, Miss Templeworth? Where is your guardian?"

His question, asked in a tone that suggested he was holding on to his temper by sheer force of will, brought Elodie up short.

"Well, I…we…my mother is—"

"Your mother is not doing her job," he interrupted smoothly. "All evening, you've been the one watching your sisters."

Elodie could only gape at him.

"How do you know?" she finally blurted, affronted by his personal questions and secretly pleased that he'd obviously been noticing her all evening.

He blinked at her question, then frowned as though confused.

"Philip told me," he said, and she felt a pang of disappointment. *Mr. Harrison. Of course.*

"Mr. Harrison should know that I do not mind watching out for my sisters," she answered defensively. "And he should know not to gossip."

Lord Brentford's answering grin was a thing of beauty, and Elodie struggled not to be distracted by it.

"'Twas merely an observation he made when I questioned him about you, Miss Templeworth. I assure you Philip wouldn't want to do anything to upset you."

Once again, Elodie was rendered speechless.

"Y-you questioned him about me?" she asked a little breathlessly, annoyed with herself for caring about what a stranger thought of her, even a tall, extremely handsome one.

"I did," he answered simply.

"But—why?" she frowned in confusion. In truth, this entire evening had been confusing.

This time his smile was smaller, crooked, and, if possible, more endearing.

"I find you fascinating, Miss Templeworth. You are without doubt one of, if not the most beautiful woman I've ever encountered, yet you seem completely unaware of the fact. And you seem to be in high demand, everybody apparently wants something from you. Yet you are unflappable. Even eighteen stones of drunk idiot doesn't rattle you."

"Oh," Elodie felt her cheeks flame with his compliments. He thought her beautiful? "Well—"

"But it is not in my nature to stand by whilst a lady is in need of assistance, I'm afraid," he continued. "And whether he meant to or not, he could have hurt you."

Elodie's heart raced at the evidence of Lord Brentford's chivalry. And though she had always prided herself on her capability and independence, it felt nice having someone look out for her. It was a rarity.

"Which goes to show you shouldn't be the one dealing with these situations. Certainly not alone."

As quickly as the warm feelings at his words appeared, they vanished again at his haughty, judgemental tone.

"I assure you, Lord Brentford, I am perfectly capable of taking care of myself *and* my sisters."

"I merely—"

"And with all due respect," she continued cutting off whatever he'd been about to say. "You don't know me or my family, and it really is none of your concern."

He stared at her for an age, his eyes glinting in the moonlight.

Finally, his mouth curved in that smile that she really didn't want to find attractive, given his high-handedness.

"To think I found you boring," he said quietly.

"I beg your pardon?" she gasped, stung by his words.

"You are correct in saying that I don't know you, of course. But I should very much like to."

Once more, his words had rendered Elodie speechless. And once more, that warm, distracting feeling blossomed in her chest.

He stepped closer, and though Elodie knew it was improper to be out here alone with a gentleman, a *stranger* no less, though she knew that he was standing far too close for propriety, she didn't step away.

She didn't even look away.

Her eyes remained captured in his blue gaze, bright even in the darkness, whilst her heart hammered almost out of her chest.

"This visit of mine has turned out to be very, very interesting," his voice was soft, hypnotic, and Elodie found herself swaying toward him.

It was all she could do to breathe as his voice drew her dangerously closer.

This was madness! This behavior was so outside of how she usually conducted herself. This was the very thing she'd run out here to prevent Cheska from doing.

And yet, she could no more move away than she could sprout wings and fly.

He reached up a hand and softly stroked her cheek.

That touch, gentle as it was, inflamed her blood, and a sort of insanity seemed to take over her.

Somewhere in the deep recesses of her mind, Elodie knew she should walk away. But he was so close and so big. His eyes were piercing her very soul. And that touch…

Elodie found herself leaning closer still, tilting her face up, delighting in the feel of his knuckles against her cheek.

He studied her for what felt like an age, his eyes intense, frowning slightly as though trying to figure her out.

Elodie didn't know what he was looking for in her gaze. She could only hope that he found it.

"Who are you, Elodie Templeworth, that you can tempt a man so?" he whispered.

Elodie had never considered herself to be a woman who could tempt a man before but oh, how she wished to be one in that moment.

Before she could even attempt to form a coherent response, Lord Brentford's lips inched closer to her own, and Elodie's head swam as a desire so potent it was staggering unfurled inside of her.

She took another, desperate step toward him, determined to leave no gap between their bodies.

She watched as his eyes lit with a fire that scorched her to her core.

Right before she abandoned all sense of decorum and threw herself into his arms, a twig beneath Elodie's slipper snapped.

The sound finally and mercifully brought Elodie back to her senses.

*Good heavens, what am I doing?* she asked herself, stumbling away from him and the spell he weaved.

As she moved away, Elodie trod on her skirts and went tumbling back.

In her panic, she reached out to grab something to break her fall.

That something was, unfortunately, Lord Brentford.

She saw his eyes widen in surprise and knew that they were both about to go tumbling to the ground.

In a flash, Lord Brentford wrapped an arm around her and turned so that she was atop him, breaking her fall and leaving her sprawled in a most unladylike fashion atop him.

They lay there, both gasping, staring into each other's eyes, and Elodie was shocked and shamed by a wanton desire to press herself closer to the rock-solid chest she could feel beneath her, to place her lips upon his own.

"I-I'm sorry, my lord," she said breathlessly, knowing she should scramble away from him yet remaining right where she was.

His grin was positively heart-stopping.

"I've been in much worse positions than this one, Miss Templeworth, believe me."

Oh, Lord, he was trouble. Not least because her body was still reacting to him in ways she'd never experienced.

Before Elodie could respond to his blatant flirtatiousness, the door to the Assembly Rooms burst open, and Mama, Hope, Francesca, and Mrs. Bell came tumbling into view.

Elodie froze right when she should have jumped to action.

She stared into the faces of her family and, of all people, the vicar's wife.

Their expressions ranged from horrified to scandalized, to rather inappropriately delighted.

And the longer Elodie lay there on top of a man in a darkened courtyard, the more reality began to seep in.

"Oh my goodness," she whispered. "I'm ruined."

# Chapter Four

T HE IRONY OF their situation was not lost on Christian as the delectable Miss Templeworth suddenly jumped to her feet, affording him the opportunity to rise to his.

By all accounts and judging from the behavior of her teara-way sisters, Miss Elodie Templeworth was the paragon of her family.

He knew it by the reverent tones Philip used when talking of the girl. By the way she kept a tight rein on her sisters, even by the way she spoke and conducted herself throughout the evening.

So yes, it was ironic that of the three beautiful Templeworth sisters in attendance tonight, Christian should find himself underneath the eldest. Not that he was complaining. Or at least, he hadn't been inclined to complain whilst her softly curved body had been pressed against his own.

Now, with her stricken expression and an avid audience, he was rather more inclined to complain.

Though he did think the young lady's whispered declaration of ruin was a trifle over-dramatic. He hadn't even had the chance to taste her. At least not yet.

It wasn't ideal that the vicar's wife was standing there looking agog. But the other ladies present were her family. And to Christian's way of thinking, the sisters were in no position to judge Miss Templeworth's behavior. Besides, her mother, had she been doing her job, could have ensured a situation such as this had never arisen in the first place. So she was in no position to judge either.

"Elodie."

Christian felt a flickering of annoyance at the older woman's stricken whisper.

Her daughter should have been inside enjoying herself. With him, preferably.

Instead, she'd been out here rescuing her sister and landing herself in trouble with a drunken lout for her efforts.

If Christian had indeed returned to the ball when she'd ordered him to, who knows what would have happened to her at the hands of that blackguard?

Probably something like this, actually.

Well, he was more than happy to take the man's place. Or he had been before they'd been rudely interrupted...

"Mama, this isn't—I didn't—"

"Why, Elodie, you sly thing. Sending me inside so you could have an assignation of your own."

Christian watched Miss Templeworth's jaw clench at her sister's gleeful declaration. She looked murderous, and, in truth, Christian didn't blame her.

Comments like that would not help to smooth over this particular bump.

"I'm impressed, Elle." This from the more flirtatious of the two blondes. "I didn't think you had it in you."

Good God, someone needed to muzzle the pair of them.

"This is not how it seems. Mrs. Bell—"

Christian turned his attention to the white-haired vicar's wife, who was gaping at Elodie Templeworth in a manner that *really* wasn't helping.

"I-I tripped, and Lord Brentford was just... That is, he... I grabbed him and—"

"You grabbed him?" Mrs. Templeworth interrupted dramatically, and Christian felt his irritation flare again.

"No!" Elodie cried. "I mean, yes but..."

She was making a mess of it.

Christian had been in far trickier situations than this. He would need to step in and fix this, so they could all go about their business.

"If I may interject—" he began, only to stop when Elodie turned a furious glare on him.

She probably wouldn't be happy that Christian's body stirred in response to the fire in those wide, chocolate eyes.

"No, you may not," she snapped, sounding nothing like the saint of insipid virtue he'd danced with only thirty minutes before.

Miss Templeworth took a deep, steadying breath before turning to face their avid audience once more.

"This whole thing is a misunderstanding," she said, her voice all decorum once more. "Mama, Mrs. Bell, you know I would never do anything that was less than respectable."

Christian watched as the two ladies exchanged a speaking look.

"That is true, Elodie. You've never given me any cause for concern," Mrs. Templeworth said softly.

"And your behavior has always been above reproach," Mrs. Bell chimed in.

Christian saw Elodie's shoulders sag, and she huffed out a sigh.

And he supposed he shouldn't feel a bit affronted by her palpable relief that she wouldn't be tied to him forever.

After all, they both knew there were only two ways something like this would end should the ladies decide that their behavior had been untoward.

A forced marriage or her complete and total ruin.

It wasn't as though he *wanted* to find himself forced into a marriage with a woman he'd only met. No matter how lovely and intriguing she was. But still. Must she be so pleased about it?

The blondes shook their heads, whispering to each other about things like "Saint Elodie" and her lucky escape.

He tried not to feel affronted by that either.

"Perhaps we should say no more about all of this," Mrs. Bell spoke again. "I'm quite sure it is best forgotten. After all, it's Elodie." She smiled kindly at the beautiful brunette, who smiled right back, looking for all the world like an angel.

But Christian had caught a glimpse of fire beneath the cool, calm surface, and it captivated him in a way that he knew he wouldn't soon forget.

"Yes, yes. Best forgotten," Elodie agreed hurriedly. "And it is getting rather late. We should return home. And...and the viscount is leaving Halton tomorrow anyway, so-so we can all just say our goodbyes and be done with it."

For the second time in his life, and both times by this conundrum of a woman before him, Christian found himself well and truly dismissed.

He frowned in consternation as she marched over and grabbed hold of her garrulous sisters, attempting to drag them away without so much of a word of goodbye. Rounding them up and hurrying them along as though they were a herd of sheep and she, their shepherdess.

Mrs. Bell made a swift retreat inside, too, he was pleased to see.

*All's well that ends well,* he told himself stoutly. After all, he had no wish to ruin the chit's life, and he absolutely had no wish to marry. Her or anyone.

He shook his head slightly, then turned to head back indoors but stopped as he caught the eye of Mrs. Templeworth.

She looked—calculating. And a sense of foreboding slithered along Christian's veins.

Christian turned the most charming smile he could muster on the lady and was rewarded with a squint that made him fear for his life.

"I do hope you have a safe journey back to wherever you came from, my lord," Elodie cried over her shoulder. "Come along, Mama," she continued, sounding all the world like the parent in their madcap family.

Christian could only laugh at the lady's non-too-subtle dismissal.

He should put this whole night, this mad town, and Miss Templeworth out of his head and head to London tomorrow just like he'd planned.

"Goodnight then," he called.

"Not so fast."

Three words.

All Mrs. Templeworth had spoken were three words, yet they brought an immediate halt to his departure.

Christian felt a flicker of annoyance as he turned back around to face the woman.

His eyes darted to the Misses Templeworths, homing in on Elodie. But she was hurrying off dragging her sisters, and he was so suspicious of the mother that he couldn't even enjoy the sway of her hips.

Much.

"My lord," Mrs. Templeworth stepped closer, a steely determination in her eyes. "I'm sure you can understand that, as my daughter's guardian, I can't very well allow this behavior to go unaddressed."

The audacity of the woman! She who left it to Elodie to parent her younger, and from what he could see, far more unruly sisters.

"My husband and I will expect you tomorrow morning. Announcements can be made after that."

Without giving him the chance to respond, Mrs. Templeworth turned on her heels and dashed off to a waiting carriage, dragging her daughters along with her.

Christian could only stare in shock, his heart thumping painfully.

Mrs. Templeworth was about as useful as a chaperone as he was as a milkmaid. Yet here, he found himself well and truly stuck.

Evidently, the lady cared less about preserving her daughter's reputation than landing herself a peer as a son-in-law.

Damn the crafty woman! She thought she had it all nicely sewn up.

Christian's anger flared as he watched the carriage trundle out of the courtyard.

So, it appeared that he had a choice.

He could allow himself to be manipulated by the scheming woman. Or he could call this situation what it was—one unfortunate incident with a girl of no consequence that he could walk away from and never think about again.

"AND HOPE SAID you were rolling about on the ground with a viscount, and I missed it."

"Sophia!"

Elodie felt her cheeks flame as twelve-year-old Sophia followed her around the garden, trampling on the rose beds and ruining Elodie's plan to ignore everything that had happened the night before.

She had very nearly ruined them all. She. Elodie. The good one. The great hope of the Templeworth family.

Elodie shuddered to think what state the family name would be in if left in the hands of Hope, Francesca, or Sophia, who even now was in breeches since she'd been riding. Not side-saddle like a lady, but astride.

Mama had given up on trying to instill any sort of ladylike behavior in Sophia. Her only hope now was that Sophia didn't disgrace them all in public. Not until at least a couple of them were married off.

"Well, is it true?" Sophia demanded now.

Elodie blew a stray lock of hair out of her eyes and turned to face her younger sister.

"No, it is most certainly *not* true," she said firmly. "I-I stumbled, and Lord Brentford very kindly helped me so that I wouldn't hurt myself."

Elodie refused to allow her mind to wander to the rock-hard strength of the man or the glint of fire in his blue eyes. Or the scent of him, the heat of him, the way she'd felt when she'd thought he might kiss her…

"And Papa is meeting with him right now."

Elodie dragged her mind from the gutter in time to hear the tail end of Sophia's ramblings.

She spun so fast that her straw bonnet flew off, unraveling the hair that she'd tucked up underneath it.

Since she was planning on hiding away until any whiff of gossip about last night died down, she hadn't bothered dressing her hair, and now it tumbled down her back. But she neither noticed nor cared.

"What do you mean?" she demanded.

For her own part, Sophia casually flicked her own plaited chestnut locks over her shoulder, shrugging nonchalantly.

"Nothing. Just that the viscount arrived some ten minutes ago and is ensconced in Papa's—Elodie!"

Elodie had turned and dashed toward the house before Sophia could finish her sentence, her basket of flowers swinging wildly with her movements.

What on earth was he doing here? Last night she had explained to both her mother and then her father, in *detail,* how nothing untoward had happened.

She had done her best to protect Francesca from either of her parents' ire during her story and had left out her reason for being in the courtyard in the first place, so it had ended up less convincing than she would have liked.

For she could give no good reason for her and Lord Brentford being alone out there.

Her story about needing some air and the viscount checking on her clearly hadn't rung true.

Mama had smugly sat back listening to Elodie's ramblings, her face the picture of disbelief.

Papa had grumbled and groused and spent more time refilling his tumbler of brandy than engaging in any sort of conversation about it.

Elodie had gone to bed feeling sick and confused but convinced that she'd managed to escape a scandal.

And if she couldn't stop remembering how it had felt to be pressed against his iron-hard chest or the feel of his impossibly strong arms wrapped around her, well then—nobody but she needed to know about it.

Now, as she ran back to the house, her heart was hammering almost out of her chest.

Why would he be here? And why on earth was he speaking to her father?

# Chapter Five

CHRISTIAN TRIED NOT to let his irritation show as he took in Mrs. Templeworth's self-satisfied expression.

Sitting in the modest study of Mr. Templeworth, he felt his cravat tightening like a noose.

*You don't need this,* he reminded himself. *The sooner you escape this madcap town and its madcap occupants, the better.*

Last night, Christian had returned to his uncle's house and confided in Philip about what had happened.

He'd left out the part where he had been on the verge of kissing the young beauty in deference to Philip's obvious regard for the girl. Yet another reason to have decided that he wouldn't be falling victim to the mother's attempts at manipulation.

Given his cousin's reaction to the tale, one would have imagined Christian had been caught tupping the girl in the garden.

His thoughts skittered away from that particular image, lest he embarrass himself in front of the lady's father, who was staring rather furiously at Christian across the cedarwood desk.

After dealing with Philip's histrionics last night, he couldn't allow himself to get into any more uncomfortable situations here. He needed to do what he came to do. Tell the Templeworths that he would not be offering for their daughter, get on his horse, and get the hell out of there.

After all, as long as the vicar's wife kept her mouth shut, they would all come out of this debacle unscathed.

He might not know much about Elodie Templeworth beyond her attractiveness and the admittedly intriguing hint of fire beneath the cool exterior, but he knew that someone as good and faultless as she didn't deserve to have her reputation ruined by one insignificant incident.

He hadn't even gotten the chance to kiss her...

But that was of no matter, of course.

"My dear, I'm sure you wish to make arrangements with Lord Brentford, so—"

Right.

This was it. Enough was enough.

"Mrs. Templeworth, I am afraid you have been laboring under an illusion. I am not here to make arrangements of any kind. I am here to tell you so there will be no misunderstanding that I will not be offering for your daughter."

His calmly spoken words seemed to freeze the very air in the room.

Mrs. Templeworth stiffened, her blue eyes glaring at him across the desk.

Elodie must have gotten those dark, sinful eyes elsewhere.

Christian shook his head slightly, refusing to get distracted by the chit's eyes. Even if she had the longest lashes he'd ever seen. Even if the color was warm, decadent, alluringly deep—

"But-but—you *ruined* her." Finally, Mrs. Templeworth broke her silence, hissing at him like a snake.

"No, I didn't," Christian answered smoothly.

He hadn't had the bloody chance to! Not that he would have, of course, he assured himself quickly.

"You will remember, madam, that your daughter explained to you what happened, and the only other witness to the unfortunate event, apart from your own family, was understanding and will be discreet, I'm sure."

"You cannot know—"

"And considering nothing untoward occurred," he continued, ignoring Mrs. Templeworth's attempt at arguing, "and that I am leaving Halton today with no plans to return, we can all forget this unfortunate incident."

Christian stood up, determined to be on his way.

Only Philip's nonsensical whining had sent him here this morning in the first place.

This was a courtesy call, so his cousin would feel comfortable around the family when next he saw them.

Christian felt sure that Philip meant to begin a courtship of the eldest Templeworth.

And, of course, that was not a twist of envy or regret in Christian's gut. He was happy for his cousin.

And the delectable Elodie.

She seemed the type who would enjoy a quiet country life, something Christian would rather stick pins in his eyes than provide.

Yet there was that flicker of feistiness in her…

"Good day to you both."

Delivering a swift bow, Christian noticed that Mr. Templeworth still hadn't moved or spoken, and his wife's entire face was turning an angry red.

"Arthur," she whispered furiously. "Aren't you going to do something?"

Christian didn't wait to see if the unusually quiet man was planning on doing something or not.

He moved swiftly from the room and into the long, mercifully quiet hallway of the Templeworth house.

It was done.

He would take his leave of his aunt and uncle. Say goodbye to his cousins and put the mad Templeworths out of his head once and for all.

Christian hurried down the hall, feeling relieved about his lucky escape and steadfastly ignoring the odd feeling in his gut when he realized he wouldn't see the bemusing, if beautiful, Miss Elodie again.

A sudden noise up ahead caught his attention, and he stopped dead as the subject of his thoughts materialized in front of him.

Her head was down, focused on the basket of roses that she clutched, giving him a glimpse of her curls spilling over her shoulders, and she seemed to be mumbling to herself as she hurried along.

Christian waited for her to look up and see him. Instead, she came barrelling closer.

Grinning slightly, he prepared for impact, reaching out to grasp her around her arms, saving her from crashing into him.

Miss Templeworth uttered a muffled "oomph" as her eyes flew up to meet his own.

Her basket of roses fell on the floor, scattering petals around their feet.

"M-my lord," she huffed as her eyes widened and her cheeks grew flushed.

And given that he'd be leaving here forever, never to return, and given the fact that he'd tossed and turned all night wondering what would have happened with her in that courtyard if her family hadn't arrived, Christian figured he had nothing to lose.

Keeping hold of Elodie, reveling in the scent that surrounded her, he pulled her gently into the darkened alcove beneath the staircase.

"Lord Brentford," she gasped. "What are you—"

Christian didn't give her a chance to finish her shocked question. He didn't give himself a chance to come to his senses or worry about Philip's reaction or even his own sanity.

Instead, he pulled Elodie Templeworth closer, cupped the nape of her neck, and captured her lips with his own.

ELODIE GASPED AS Lord Brentford's lips descended upon her.

*What on earth is going on here?* she thought to herself.

The man had clearly run mad. Or-or perhaps he considered

them to be engaged?

After all, he had been leaving the house having met with her father…

Her thoughts were becoming more muddled as sensation began to take over her body.

But this would not do!

She couldn't allow herself to stand here and be kissed by this man. Not least because she had no idea *why* they were kissing.

Elodie gathered what was left of her lauded decorum and placed her hands upon his chest, determined to push him away.

*Oh heavens.*

He was rock solid. The muscle beneath her palms was hard and rigid and blisteringly hot, even beneath the lawn shirt and waistcoat.

Lord Brentford angled his head, slanting his mouth across her own once again, and Elodie found herself not pushing him away but moving her hands upward to twine around his neck.

His groan of approval shattered the last of her hesitation, and she pressed herself wantonly against him.

"Open for me, sweetheart," he whispered against her lips before his tongue darted out to trace the seam of her lips.

Elodie gasped all over again as his actions seemed to scorch her very blood, and he took advantage of the movement by delving that wicked tongue inside of her mouth.

Elodie was lost, caught in pure sensation, and she couldn't contain the moan that seemed to come from the very depths of her soul.

She could do nothing but cling to him as the tempest he awakened raged within her.

His hands moved, blazing a path down her body, to grab her and pull her impossibly closer. He moved them, turning so her back was pressed against the wall, her front to his heated frame.

And still, Elodie could only hang on for dear life, her hands tangled in his hair.

When Lord Brentford ripped his mouth from her own, she

couldn't stem the sound of protest, but before reality could pierce the haze of her desperation, his mouth moved to her neck, licking the wildly fluttering pulse, nipping the sensitive flesh.

"Christ, Elodie." The tortured desperation in his voice was matched only by what she was feeling, and—

"Elodie!"

Elodie froze as Sophia's voice rang out down the hallway.

Lord Brentford's gaze snapped up to meet her own, and her skin heated all over again at the blue fire that lit their depths.

"Elle?"

Elodie panicked as her famed, but clearly unreliable common sense returned, and she shoved ineffectually against his broad, solid chest.

"Move," she hissed. "Quickly."

He stepped back, and she darted out of the alcove and threw herself on the floor beside the basket, desperately throwing the ruined roses and petals back in with abandon.

What on earth had she been thinking? What had she been *doing?* Her cheeks scalded, even as that molten desire he'd awoken still slid along her veins.

She needed him to leave. She needed to be able to breathe, and think, and—

"Allow me."

Suddenly, he was kneeling beside her, and her poor, over-worked senses were battered again by the scent of him, the proximity of him.

"My lord, you—ouch!"

Elodie glanced down as a thorn from one of the roses pierced her finger, though thankfully, it didn't break the skin.

Even as she frowned at the offending flower, Lord Brentford's large, gloveless hand plucked the bloom from her fingers, and then, presumably with the intention of finishing her off once and for all, he lifted the injured finger to his mouth.

"Don't," she hissed, but even she could hear the need for him that still colored her tone.

With a devilish smile, he leaned down and licked the digit. There, kneeling in the hallway, where anyone could happen upon them.

"Elle, there you are. What are you—oh."

Sophia's appearance had Elodie wrenching herself from Lord Brentford's grip and darting to her feet.

She stared into the assessing eyes of her little sister, desperately hoping that she looked a lot calmer than she felt.

She felt rather than saw Lord Brentford stand slowly to his impressive height beside her.

Sophia's narrowed eyes traveled from Elodie to the viscount and back again.

"Sophia," Elodie dragged her unruly body and heart back under control. "Allow me to present Lord Brentford. My lord, my younger sister, Miss Sophia Templeworth." Her voice was as wobbly as her knees, but there was nothing she could do about that, only brazen it out.

His lordship, on the other hand, seemed insultingly unaffected by what had just happened and delivered an elegant bow to her sister.

"An honor, Miss Templeworth," he drawled, all charm and politeness.

Sophia snorted in a most unladylike fashion, but Elodie couldn't bring herself to scold. Nor could she bring herself to be scandalized by Sophia's appearing in front of a peer of the realm, wearing breeches. She had far too many thoughts to contend with as it was.

"So, have you come to propose to my sister?"

Elodie gaped in horror at Sophia's forthrightness. Although she had to admit to herself, she was rather interested in the answer.

"Sophia," she admonished. But her heart wasn't in it.

She could feel Lord Brentford's eyes on her, and she turned to meet his assessing gaze.

He frowned slightly as though there was some confusing

thought on his mind.

But after a time, the confusion cleared, and he looked— contrite.

"No, Miss Templeworth," he answered Sophia's question but kept his eyes trained on Elodie. "I'm afraid I've come to say goodbye."

# Chapter Six

CHRISTIAN HURRIED FROM the Templeworth house and the temptation of Elodie.

He tried to shake off the remnants of the lust she'd awoken in him. Just as he tried to shake off the guilt he felt when he'd looked into those damned deep, brown eyes.

Perhaps he shouldn't have kissed her, knowing he was going to be walking away from her.

Perhaps he should have guessed that a kiss between them would have been that explosive and very nearly impossible to walk away from.

Though, truthfully, he never could have imagined the strength of its impact.

But Christian wasn't the marrying kind. And when he did eventually marry, it wouldn't be to a paragon of goodness and decorum.

He'd be bored senseless within a week.

And yet…

The idea of being bored around Elodie Templeworth with those eyes…and those lips…and those moans as he'd taken her mouth with his own…

*Christ.* Christian's body stirred to life again at the mere memory of that encounter.

He couldn't remember a single time he'd been so close to losing control as when he'd been holding Elodie Templeworth in his arms.

He'd been seconds from lifting the girl's skirts. In her father's house. In a bloody hallway.

All the more reason to get the hell out of there.

Yet when her sister, another hoyden in breeches of all things, with chestnut tresses the same color as her sister's, had questioned him so forwardly about his intentions, looking into Elodie's eyes, the taste of her still upon his lips, the floral scent of her still clinging to his skin, he'd momentarily been tempted to offer for her there and then.

And when a semblance of logic had mercifully returned, and he'd confessed that he had no intention toward the lady, damned if guilt didn't hit him like a punch to the gut.

It was those eyes. They were so deep, so trusting.

*Ah hell.*

Well, it was done now. He'd taken his leave of the girl, ignoring her sister's assessing gaze and the small, insane part of him that desperately wanted to stay by her side.

When he got to Town, he'd pay a visit to Cressida.

He'd had a longstanding arrangement with the young, beautiful widow for years, and it suited him. Allowed him to slake his lust without any pressure or expectation.

Cressida was as in love with Christian as he was with her, which was to say not at all.

The willowy, red-haired, blue-eyed beauty had married up and married young. So when her elderly husband shuffled off the mortal coil, she'd been left with money, status, and freedom that simply wasn't available to young, single ladies of the *ton*.

Yes, he'd head straight to Cressida's.

The Season hadn't started yet, but Cressida never left London.

He'd see his mistress and get his equilibrium back.

And if red hair and blue eyes suddenly seemed a poor substitute for chestnut curls and chocolate-brown eyes, well then, he'd just have to live with that.

Christian made light work of mounting his stallion Ares and was soon traveling to the inn where he'd agreed to meet Philip.

He doffed his hat to the smattering of people whom he encountered on the way, frowning as they scowled back at him or whispered behind their gloves.

Odd. He'd considered Halton quite a friendly place.

The closer he got to the village, the more Christian's confusion grew, and a prickling of unease ran along his skin.

There were ladies openly glaring at him now, ladies who'd fawned over him not twenty-four hours before. And he could feel the hostility coming off the village folk in waves.

*What the hell is going on now?* he thought, more desperate than ever to get as far away from this place as possible.

Reaching the inn, Christian rushed inside to seek out Philip.

At least there'd be one friendly face in the crowd of this sudden unfriendliness.

Spotting his cousin slouched over a tankard at a corner table, Christian moved quickly to take a seat opposite him.

"Philip," he sighed in relief. "I swear this place gets odder by the second. I think—"

"It's out."

Christian stopped talking at Philip's cryptic, morose interruption.

"What?" he frowned in confusion.

He looked properly at Philip now. Two angry splotches of color stained his cousin's rounded cheeks, and he was staring glumly into his ale as though the answer to all of life's questions were contained within the amber brew.

"It's. Out."

Christian bit back a curse of irritation. Philip wasn't always the most open of men, and it wasn't his cousin's fault that Christian's mind was still on the doe-eyed Miss Prim he'd just left, who turned out to have something not at all innocent lurking under the surface…

"You'll have to elaborate, I'm afraid," Christian's smile felt strained, but he kept it plastered to his face.

Finally, Philip looked up, his eyes boring into Christian's.

"The whole village is talking of it, Christian. Your—encounter with Elodie. That is, Miss Templeworth."

Christian's gut twisted, and for one mad moment, he thought his cousin, and indeed this inconsequential little place, somehow knew of his kiss with Elodie.

But, of course, Philip was talking of the non-event from last night.

"What?" Christian said now, leaning forward to glare at his cousin. "How?" he demanded. "And nothing bloody happened," he tacked on for good measure.

"I don't know how," he answered despondently. "And I believe you. But well, the way the story is being told—it doesn't sound all that innocent, does it?"

Christian felt vaguely shamed as he thought of what the very proper, very decorous Miss Templeworth would suffer when she heard that she was being gossiped about. When she heard that her reputation was in tatters.

*Only, she's not all that proper, is she? Not when she's coming undone in your arms.*

Christian ignored the voice in his head.

He swallowed hard.

Why had he bloody well gone to see Templeworth? Why hadn't he just gone straight to Town? If he were currently en route to London, he wouldn't know about this catastrophe. He would be blissfully unaware of the plight of Miss Templeworth. But then, he'd never have known the pleasure of her, warm and pliant in his arms.

A small price to pay, however, if the alternative was this.

"You'll have to pay a call," Philip continued in that irritating, despondent voice.

"I *did* pay a call," Christian said through gritted teeth, aware that the whole room was avidly watching their exchange. "I explained to the chit's father that nothing untoward happened, and I explained to her grasping mother that I wouldn't be marrying Miss Templeworth."

Philip stared at him for what felt like an age, and Christian felt his cravat tightening like a noose.

Finally, however, his cousin spoke again.

"I'm sure that once you return and explain, the lady will accept your offer."

Christian's heart thudded painfully as guilt vied with frustration within him.

The lady would be fine.

She was beloved in this small part of the country. And here was Philip, Christian's own cousin, completely enamored of the girl.

Christian didn't *want* to get married.

That made him an utterly selfish bastard, true. But they'd all get over this in time.

Gads, if he could up and leave now, he would. Only he'd stupidly told his driver that they wouldn't leave until tomorrow morning. He'd known the man had family in the area and had decided to magnanimously allow him a couple of days to visit with them. So he was stuck.

Even if he sent word that he'd changed his mind, it would take time for the driver to return and for his valet Simmons to ready everything for the journey. Though he could insist that Simmons set off later this evening with his trunks whilst he awaited the arrival of his personal conveyance and driver.

Perhaps he would just jump straight back on Ares and allow his valet and carriage to follow him.

A more uncomfortable journey, no doubt. But infinitely preferable to the nightmare currently unfolding.

"You care for her, don't you, Philip?" Christian asked now, his eyes narrowed on his cousin's features.

Everything about Philip was plain. Simple.
*And nothing about Elodie is.*
But that was irrelevant.

Philip opened and closed his mouth like a fish, so Christian pressed on.

"And you know there is no truth in these ugly rumors."

"What's your point, Christian?" Philip asked, a frown of confusion stamped on his face.

"Well," Christian continued carefully, watching Philip's reactions. "You—that is she—" He blew out a frustrated breath. "It's not as though the girl would be without options. You wouldn't let something like this stop you from paying your addresses, for example."

Once more, Philip put Christian in mind of a fish out of water.

Before he could congratulate himself on sewing things up rather nicely and appeasing his guilt, however, his damned brain conjured images of Elodie walking down the aisle toward Philip. Her soft, pink lips being tasted by Philip. Her sinful body against Philip, beneath Philip. And the jealousy would have knocked him on his arse were he not already sitting.

What madness was this? They'd shared one kiss. One.

"You would pass her off as though she means nothing?" Philip demanded now, showing the first glimpse of any sort of strength Christian had seen from him. "You would treat her as though she is an inconvenience to be dealt with by someone else? By me? Whilst you flit back to your bronzed, Town bachelorhood?"

Philip's words only heightened the guilt that Christian was feeling, and he squirmed uncomfortably.

Before the diatribe could continue, the serving girl who had been more than a little friendly to Christian since his arrival in Halton appeared with a tray and two tankards.

She placed one in front of the still scowling Philip, and rather than slide one to Christian, leaning over to give him an excellent view of her abundant assets as had been her wont, she slammed the other tankard in front of him, sloshing the liquid out onto the table before stalking off with her nose in the air.

It would seem even the serving wenches had a soft spot for Miss Templeworth.

Philip climbed to his feet, straightening his shoulders to presumably make the most of his rather unimpressive height.

"I would not have the lady treated so ill. So, you are correct. I will do right by her for the sake of this family, and because," here his face became an alarming shade of puce, "because she's—that is I have come to—"

"Spit it out, Philip," Christian snapped, unease at Philip's words slithering through his veins, this baffling jealousy heating his blood.

Philip merely stared at him before shaking his head and marching out of the pub.

With a black oath, Christian threw some coins on the table. Far more than necessary, as a matter of fact, not that the ungrateful wretches here would appreciate that, and stomped out after his cousin.

There would be no calling at his aunt's house. No friendly goodbyes to the vicar and his wife.

He was getting the hell away from here and had no plans to set foot in any residence of Halton ever again.

Especially not Miss Elodie Templeworth's.

# Chapter Seven

ELODIE COULD FEEL her legs shaking under her dimity gown. The tense silence of the drawing room made her feel nauseous, but she didn't know how to break it.

She'd said everything that needed to be said. She'd begged. She'd pleaded. She'd cried at the injustice and laughed at the ludicrousness.

And it was no use.

Mama, for reasons known only to herself, would not be prevailed upon to be reasonable.

She alternated between caterwauling about Elodie's ruination, about how she had been their only hope, about how if she didn't become the Viscountess Brentford, hell and damnation would rain down on the Templeworth name.

It was all very loud and silly.

Papa had finally opened his mouth enough to at least try to quieten his wife's concerns.

But it wasn't doing any good. Mama wouldn't stop bemoaning their lot in life.

"Elodie," she wailed for the hundredth time. "You were the *good* one. The one on whom we pinned all our hopes. If you cannot marry the man who ruined you, what chance do any of my girls have?"

*Oh, for heaven's sake.*

Elodie worked hard to school her features, lest her face give away her thoughts.

She simply couldn't understand Mama's attitude. And frankly, her mind was so muddled from her explosive encounter with Lord Brentford earlier that she didn't really have the sense required to figure it all out.

"Mama," she tried again. "You forget that nobody *knows* about this. Nobody apart from Mrs. Bell, who has assured us that she will be discreet. If that lady can have faith in me, why can't you?"

Before Mama could answer, a knock sounded on Papa's door, and their butler Figgins entered, his expression blank as always, even though he and the rest of the household must have heard all of Mama's lamentations.

"Mr. Harrison to see you, sir."

For one wild moment, Elodie thought it might be Christian come back. But, of course, he was Lord Brentford, not merely Mr. Harrison.

Papa frowned at Mama.

"Philip Harrison?" he asked quietly.

"Lord Brentford is Mr. Harrison's cousin, Papa," Elodie answered quietly since Mama was scowling at the doorway and paying no heed to either of them.

Papa sighed and rolled his eyes.

"This is becoming farcical," he bit out, unusually surly. "Very well, Figgins. Send him in."

Figgins bowed deferentially then moved away to do Papa's bidding.

"Perhaps he's here to make amends," Papa said soothingly to Mama. "After all, if the viscount won't see Elodie right—"

"Papa," Elodie interrupted, a sort of panic fluttering along her nerves. "There truly is nothing to make amends *for*."

Her mind flashed to the kiss with Lord Brentford in the hallway. His body pressed insistently against her, his mouth hot and desperate upon her own.

But she brutally pushed the memory away.

She was absolutely sure nobody knew about *that*.

It would be her secret. Her wicked, delicious secret—

"And if he does want to marry her, well, she could do worse, I suppose."

Elodie got her wanton thoughts under control in time to hear the tail end of Papa's sentiment, and she went cold.

Before she could object, however, Mama scoffed.

"Worse?" she bit out. "He is a *farmer*, Arthur. A farmer. Lord Brentford is a peer of the realm."

"Yes, and he's gone. Mr. Harrison is of good standing and is a wealthy, *gentleman* farmer. You've always liked Mrs. Harrison and her children."

Mama reached up to pinch the bridge of her nose.

"Arthur, do you realize the opportunity before us? A *viscount*. Can you imagine the doors that will open for our family? For our girls?"

"Catherine, he's *gone*," Papa snapped obviously as fed up with this ridiculous argument as Elodie was.

For her part, she had been completely forgotten by both her parents. As though it wasn't her life they were sitting there discussing.

Her emotions, as she sat quietly, were riotous.

Terrified that she would find herself married to Philip, who, while a perfectly pleasant sort of man, wasn't someone she'd envisioned spending her life with.

And most of all, annoyed by the *frisson* of disappointment that Lord Brentford had kissed her like that, then walked away without a backward glance.

She shook her head slightly to dispel the foolish thoughts.

Had it really only been a day since her life had been perfectly fine? Now it was in chaos.

And all because of that giant, arrogant cad who'd swooped in, caused complete havoc, and swooped back out again.

"Let's just hear Harrison out. If this has been kept quiet as Elodie claims, then we don't have anything to worry about.

Perhaps he's only here to make his apologies for his cousin's behavior."

"Don't be foolish Arthur. I—"

"If he offers for her," Papa continued, refusing to allow Mama to interrupt. "I'll only consider it if it suits."

Anger, swift and fierce, rose up inside Elodie.

*Suits who?* She wanted to yell. *Do I not get a say?*

But, of course, she swallowed it down and said nothing. She was the good one, after all.

Hope would never allow herself to be talked about as though she weren't there.

Francesca would demand the opportunity to pick her own husband.

Sophia would sooner burn the house to ash than even allow such a conversation to happen after one non-event in a practically empty courtyard, though, of course, she was still too young for such things.

But Elodie—she wasn't the type to complain. Even if her parents decided she should marry a man for whom she felt nothing but lukewarm friendship.

Even if they were planning a life for her that she didn't particularly want.

She was the well-behaved daughter. She wouldn't resist. And she wouldn't complain.

The sound of approaching footsteps brought a cessation to her parents' hushed conversation and heralded the arrival of Mr. Harrison, who appeared behind Figgins and was mopping his profusely sweating brow.

"Mr. Harrison, come in," Papa called, standing to greet the man.

Philip's eyes darted to Elodie, who stood and curtsied, then back to Papa.

"Mr. Templeworth, Mrs. Templeworth." Philip bowed to Elodie's parents. "Miss Templeworth," he added almost as an afterthought, sketching a quick bow in Elodie's direction. "I have come to discuss, that is to ask that—well—ah—"

"You are here on behalf of your cousin, the viscount?"

Elodie felt a flicker of annoyance at Mama's presumptuous question, given that only an hour ago, Lord Brentford had spelled out that he had no intentions toward her.

Though that explosive kiss had made it seem like perhaps…

"N-no, Mrs. Templeworth. Sadly, my cousin is set to depart tomorrow morning at first light and will not be returning to the area."

Elodie could see that Mama was gearing up for some more hysterics, so she spoke up. Something of an anomaly for her.

"But there is no harm done," she blurted. "Since nothing untoward took place between the viscount and me. *And,*" she continued when all three occupants of the room opened their mouths to speak. "Nobody knows."

"Ah—as to that…" Philip spoke, and Elodie's stomach dropped as she noted the profuse sweating again, the scarlet splotches on his cheeks. "I'm-I'm afraid that it seems word has gotten out. There is—er—*talk*. A lot of speculation."

Elodie could only stare in horror as her stomach dropped to her toes.

It wasn't just that Mama was surely seconds away from an all-out fit of the vapors. Or that Papa would be gruffly disappointed. Or that she had quite possibly ruined her sisters' prospects— ironic given that none of their own behaviors had done so thus far.

It wasn't even the injustice of being accused of something that she *didn't do*. At least, not in the courtyard.

No. It was that Elodie dedicated every waking moment of her life to being good. Pure and kind, and above reproach. Yet it was she who stood here now, hearing that her reputation was in tatters, hearing that the friendships she'd built and the reputation she had cultivated was all for naught.

Ruined by a handsome viscount who'd kissed her then left her, without so much as a backward glance.

She'd been undone by a blackguard, and now her life was ruined.

Like clockwork, Mama's tantrum began, and her screeching reached levels Elodie wouldn't have believed a human was capable of making.

"It's not as bad as all that, dear," Papa was shouting about the racket. "I'm sure it will all blow over in time. She can go and stay with my sister in Bath and—"

"I-if I may?" Elodie winced as Philip's loud stuttering joined the fray. This was becoming painfully absurd.

She looked to the window in the hopes of climbing out and escaping and was less than amused to see Hope, Francesca, and Sophia's faces squashed against the glass, all of them agog at her misfortune.

"If I may?" Philip's voice had risen now to a veritable bellow.

Elodie felt her cheeks heat as she watched the display before her and tried to ignore the snickering that she knew was taking place outside the window.

Though she might at times grow frustrated with her sisters, generally speaking, she wasn't given to fits of anger.

Yet standing there in the midst of the cacophony of cries and yells and screeches, she felt like tearing her hair out.

"I have a proposed solution," Philip roared at Mama now.

His roar at least served to quieten Mama's caterwauling. The cessation of noise was abrupt and left Elodie's ears ringing.

A solution, Philip had said. As though Elodie's life was a problem to be solved.

She frowned in confusion as he mopped his brow again, huffing out a breath and turning to speak to her father.

"I-I understand that my cousin's behavior has been less than appropriate, sir. And I am conscious of the potential damage to poor Miss Templeworth's excellent reputation."

"It's not your fault, Mr. Harrison," Elodie interrupted, a vague feeling of discomfort piercing the hot anger and calming her somewhat. She didn't know why this conversation was starting to fill her with dread, but it was. Perhaps it was because she suspected he was here to offer for her, just as Papa had said. "And really, there's no need to—"

"Let the man speak, Elodie."

Elodie dutifully quietened at her father's sharp command, silently stewing and wondering what on earth was going to happen to her.

The people here had known Elodie her whole life. Knew her character. Knew how she conducted herself.

Surely whatever gossip was flying about couldn't be so bad as to undo twenty years of goodness.

She felt hurt that Mrs. Bell—whom she had helped for years in whatever capacity was required—would share the unfortunate incident in the courtyard, when she'd promised that she wouldn't.

"How bad is it, Harrison?" Papa indicated that Philip should sit in the chair beside Elodie's.

She turned to look out the window, but her sisters were gone. Had probably scarpered when Papa had snapped at her. Their father didn't often raise his voice, but when he did, the younger three always had the good sense to run.

Elodie had never had to. The fact that it was she who'd angered him this time made her stomach flip with the unfairness of it, but she dared not say so.

"You know how these things go, Mr. Templeworth," Philip spoke in dire tones. "What started off as something innocuous has become something quite scandalous."

Mama's whimper of distress was most unhelpful.

"I must stress, sir, that I believe your daughter to be completely innocent of any wrongdoing." Philip turned to smile at Elodie, but she couldn't muster one to return. "And as I said, I am very conscious of the duty that my family owes to yours to rectify the damage done to your lovely daughter."

There was a brief pause while Philip took a breath, Mama dabbed at her cheeks with a lace handkerchief, and Papa steepled his fingers.

Elodie felt frozen to the spot.

"Therefore, I would like to off—"

"No!"

For a moment, Elodie was confused, wondering who had shouted. Then she realized she was on her feet, and it had been her.

The other occupants stared at her in varying degrees of shock and displeasure.

"I-I—"

She didn't know what to say. She'd never been at the receiving end of censure, and she'd certainly never done anything so bold as to jump to her feet and yell out an objection. To anything.

"Leave us."

Before she could think of a thing to say, Papa spoke. His tone brooked no argument. Yet Elodie couldn't simply walk away and allow her life to be decided whilst she wasn't even in the room.

They must all know what Philip was here for. Just as Elodie knew that it wasn't what she wanted.

But years of being bred to be seen and not heard, to never displease her elders, and to always mind her tongue and her manners were hard to shake, and Elodie found herself helplessly doing as she was bid.

"Shut the door on your way out," her father intoned firmly.

The thud of the door sounded like a death knell as Elodie pulled it to.

This was it, then.

Philip would be her husband.

She would never leave Halton.

Odd that she'd always assumed she would stay here happily yet, now that such a fate was being decided for her, the beloved village felt more like a prison than a home.

Foolish to cry over something such as this. Marrying Philip would ensure a respectable life. The scandal would die down soon enough—especially when her betrothal was announced.

And her sisters would be spared any ill-treatment because of her.

Elodie lifted her fingers to press against the lips that just that morning had been pressed against Lord Brentford's.

Marrying Philip might not have seemed so bad before she'd met the viscount. Before she'd experienced true pleasure, real desire. Before his one kiss had made her quite certain that she'd never find Philip attractive.

But now that she *had* felt the touch of his lips, she would always know what she was missing.

And the future currently being planned for her seemed boring. Empty. Miserable.

She had staunchly denied it, but to herself, at least, she must be truthful.

Viscount Brentford *had* ruined her.

Just not in the way her family imagined.

# Chapter Eight

"YOU CANNOT MEAN to accept Philip blasted Harrison's suit, Elle."

Elodie couldn't even rouse her spirits to tell Sophia to watch her language.

She'd thought that sitting on the swing she'd played on as a girl would gain her some peace and solitude.

But, of course, she didn't account for the fact that the swing could be seen from the stables, and that unless it was the middle of the night, Sophia would be in the stables.

"Just tell them no."

"You found her, then?"

Elodie looked up from her slippers at the arrival of Hope, whose brown eyes so like her own were filled with concern.

"She didn't even scold me," Sophia whispered.

"Well, you know you can't marry him," Hope said matter-of-factly as though Elodie had a choice.

"Bad enough that you'd saddle yourself with one man but Philip Harrison?" She shuddered and flicked a curl over her shoulder.

Despite Elodie's best efforts, she'd never been able to make any of her sisters wear their hair up unless they were in company. They cared not that visitors would see their hair undressed. Elodie had hastily pinned her own hair before being summoned to Papa's study.

*If you keep lecturing me, I'll wear the rest of me undressed, too,* Francesca had once threatened. And Elodie had backed off because, in truth, she wouldn't trust Cheska not to follow through on her threat.

"Now, if it was his delicious cousin, the viscount, I might understand."

At the mention of Lord Brentford, Elodie's heart stuttered, and try as she might, she couldn't stop remembering how it felt to be locked in his impossibly strong embrace, to have her whole body set aflame with his kiss—

"Elle? What's wrong with her?"

This time Elodie didn't need to look up. She knew it was Francesca by the demanding voice.

"What do you think is wrong with her?" Hope drawled. "She's afraid she's going to have to marry that pig farmer. And where have you been?"

"I've been eavesdropping, of course," Cheska answered swiftly. "And I can tell you that unless you do something about it, Elodie, you *will* have to marry the pig farmer. Even now, he and Papa are discussing marriage contracts and quick ceremonies to limit the damage."

It wasn't news to her; she had suspected as much after all. But still, Elodie's stomach roiled, and panic skittered along her veins.

"Nothing even happened," she croaked desperately. "I don't know how everyone knows. I don't know *what* everyone knows."

"Well," Cheska spoke in her usual blunt manner, "According to the farmer, the rumors floating around about you make Hope look positively angelic."

Hope merely shrugged, completely unconcerned that people may think her a scandalous wanton.

For Elodie, it was her worst nightmare.

"It's not fair," she whispered. "We didn't—I didn't—"

"No, it's not fair," Cheska interrupted. "Especially since I feel responsible. After all, if I hadn't been out there halfway to being foxed, *you* wouldn't have been out there with the dashing viscount."

Elodie appreciated her sisters' support, but she wished they'd offer it without constantly referring to Lord Brentford's handsomeness. She was already far too distracted by the memory of his kiss.

She didn't need constant reminders of his chiseled jaw or his piercing blue eyes or that wicked smile…

"And that's why I'm going to help you fix it," Cheska announced, finally grabbing Elodie's full attention.

"Fix it?" she repeated in confusion. "How can we fix it? If people think I-I–well, that I allowed Lord Brentford to take liberties—and now the man has disappeared—then I have no choice but to accept Mr. Harrison's kind offer. He does me a great service by trying to help salvage our family name."

Sophia's sound of disgust was matched only by Hope's snort of derision.

"Kind offer, indeed." Her dark eyes flashed dangerously. "Great service? Elle, he's been salivating over you for years. I'm sure he jumped at the chance to use this unfortunate incident to trap you."

"Mmhmm. I would bet my horse that he spread the rumors himself," Sophia spat, her eyes sparking with a matching fury.

"I'm sure that's not true," Elodie answered weakly.

Surely Philip wouldn't be so unkind? So devious.

But then, she reasoned, she never would have imagined that Mrs. Bell would be so unkind either.

Her head was beginning to ache with her circuitous thoughts.

"That's because you assume everyone is as good as you, and they're not," Hope said stoutly. "How can you be the eldest and still the most innocent?"

Once again, Elodie's mind darted to her encounter with the viscount.

That had been the furthest thing from innocent Elodie had ever experienced.

Though nobody knew.

Unlike the courtyard with its grossly exaggerated incident, the real scandal, the kiss that had set fire to her from head to toe, was a secret between her and the viscount.

"It is not innocence," she insisted, deliberately removing thoughts of Lord Brentford from her head. "It's pragmatism."

"It's foolish," Cheska interrupted darkly.

"Well, what would you have me do?" Elodie snapped, the anger she'd felt in Papa's office suddenly making itself known again. "Even if Mr. Harrison were using my disgrace as an opportunity, which I don't believe he would do, he's still offering a way out of this mess. Offering you all a chance to enter the marriage mart with your reputations stain-free. You cannot underestimate the value of such an offer."

"Any damage to my reputation will be done by me and me alone, thank you very much." Hope was typically cavalier about her flirtatious nature.

"And I wouldn't want a husband so weak that he'd be put off by a mere whiff of scandal that didn't even involve me," Francesca said.

"Boys are disgusting in any case," Sophia shrugged.

"You are free to think boys are disgusting because you are young, Sophia. But in time, you will understand the importance of these things in a way that Hope and Francesca refuse to."

If she'd hoped her censure would have any effect on her strong-willed sisters, she was disappointed by their nonchalant shrugs.

"Personally, I think the entire thing is ridiculous. Even if everyone in Halton is speaking ill of you, which I highly doubt given how virtuous you are, it's a tiny village of no consequence to anyone. How would anyone outside of the area even know about it?"

"Papa wanted to send me to Bath, Hope. He doesn't seem to care that it won't have reached the ears of anyone outside of the village. And even if he did, Mama certainly won't let it be forgotten."

"But–but to get married? Marriage is permanent, Elodie. Once you do it, there's no going back. Unless he dies. But he seems annoyingly healthy."

"Wait—Bath? To Aunt Mildred?" Cheska asked, interrupting Hope's rather concerning words about Mr. Harrison.

Elodie could only nod miserably. "I cannot think that marriage to Philip would be worse than that."

"Even I might be tempted to marry the pig farmer if it kept me away from Mildred and her lecherous husband," Francesca shuddered in disgust.

"Hmm. And our odious cousins," Hope interjected most unhelpfully. "Don't you recall Reginald's wandering hands when he's in his cups? Which is most of the time, Elle. You simply cannot go there."

Elodie jumped up from the swing, suddenly too agitated to sit still.

"I cannot marry Philip. I cannot go to Bath. You're all very good at telling me what I *shouldn't* do, but none of you seem to know what I *should* do," she said in exasperation.

"You should do nothing," Hope said immediately. "Brazen it out and bide your time. Not much goes on here, granted. But eventually, somebody else will cause a scandal, and yours will be quite forgotten. Most likely me, come to think of it."

"You causing a scandal won't exactly undo any damage to the family name, Hope," Elodie said dryly.

"You should march in there and tell Papa, Mr. Harrison, and anyone else who cares to know that you will *not* be martyring yourself into a loveless marriage. That you don't care for their judgments or silly opinions."

Elodie would give anything for even a fraction of Francesca's steely spirit and courage.

Sadly, those were things in which she very much came up short.

"I cannot bear to be the subject of gossip," she whispered, a lump in her throat. "And I certainly cannot go in there and defy father so vocally."

"So, that's it? You're going to be sent away or forced to marry the farmer while the viscount gets to leave with no consequences? It hardly seems fair."

Sophia's quietly spoken words silenced her older sisters, and they stood in contemplative quiet, each of them caught up in her own thoughts.

For Elodie, the effect of Sophia's words was swift and severe.

The anger that had bubbled under her skin in Papa's study roared to vociferous life.

Sophia was quite right.

She hadn't *done* anything. Even in the hallway, *he* had kissed *her*.

Her innate honesty meant she had to admit to herself that she'd kissed him right back. But he'd started it.

And now he was relaxing at the inn before he went on his merry way to Town, leaving her behind to suffer the consequences.

It was the outside of enough.

The anger burned and roiled inside of her.

She looked from Hope's face to Francesca's, to Sophia's.

All of them looked at her as though she were going to the gallows.

And all of them looked at her that way because they knew she would never take on board their suggestions.

She wouldn't be brazen like Hope, or forthright like Francesca, or brave like Sophia.

She would quietly stand by whilst everyone decided her life for her, and what's more, she'd thank them for the privilege.

Suddenly Elodie's future flashed before her eyes. A quiet, unassuming, uneventful, boring existence with Mr. Harrison, or a miserable, potentially dangerous life in Aunt Mildred's Bath residence, filled with wandering hands and lecherous relatives.

And then her mind flitted to the viscount, and her heart stuttered with remembered excitement even as her anger still stormed inside of her.

He owed her nothing, Elodie knew.

And she couldn't blame him for walking away. Nor could she regret that he'd kissed her because it had been the single most exhilarating thing she'd ever experienced.

But at the same time, it was really quite beyond the pale that she alone should pay the price of their unfortunate meeting.

It wasn't that she wanted him to suffer alongside her. She wanted *neither* of them to suffer.

A movement by the house caught Elodie's eye, and she saw that Mrs. Stevens, the most loose-lipped lady in all of Halton, had arrived and was rushing toward the front door.

Heavens, when Mama heard that lady's gossip, she'd have Elodie married before anyone could say "'overreaction." Philip, Elodie was sure, would suddenly become a palatable match when faced with Mrs. Stevens' vicious tongue.

"Mrs. Stevens," Hope's dire tone matched Elodie's mood. "Well, that's that, Elle. Once she sees Mr. Harrison here and puts two and two together, the news of your betrothal will be all over town."

As tempted as Elodie was to defy whatever her father was deciding in that house, she knew she'd never put a stop to it when the entirety of Halton knew. Especially if it meant humiliating poor Philip.

She'd be forced to marry him.

The only way she wouldn't be was if she wasn't here.

The thought popped into Elodie's head, and her whole body stiffened.

*No.*

Immediately, she shied away from it.

But a tiny part of her, the small, secret part that had thrilled in the arms of the viscount, that had done something truly scandalous, that had misbehaved for the first time in her adult life—that part wouldn't be silenced.

*You can't marry him if you're not here.*

It was madness. Complete foolishness to even be thinking it.

Yet the voice wouldn't be silenced.

*And they can't send you away to Bath if you've already left Halton.*

But—but Elodie wasn't the type to run. Her entire body went cold when she thought of the scandal it would cause.

And yet…

Try as she might, she couldn't seem to silence that rebellious part of her that said it could easily be explained away.

A letter saying she was sorry, but she couldn't stay here.

A story told to their friends and neighbors, saying she was gone to stay with a relative. Their aunt, perhaps. In Bath.

It would be that simple. Nobody would need to know otherwise.

And though Papa would be furious and Mama distraught, at least Elodie would be free.

*No,* she told herself even more sternly this time. *You cannot galivant about the place alone. What are you thinking?*

Even the unexpectedly rebellious part of her agreed with that. Not only was it ruinous, but it was dangerous, too. She might be an innocent, but she knew enough of the world to know what could befall a young lady alone in it.

And where would she go in any case? She certainly would *not* go to their Aunt Mildred in Bath.

She didn't have many options.

Although she argued with herself some more, it would be time for the entire family to remove to the London house soon.

What harm if she were to get there a few weeks early? She wouldn't go out and about. She wouldn't be seen by anyone in their circle.

But it was familiar. A home away from home. Not yet fully open, there was still a skeletal staff. More than enough people to take care of Elodie, and she could help them open it for the Season…

Her mind whirled with possibilities. Possibilities that before last night she wouldn't have even dreamed of.

Going to London for a few weeks before her family solved all of her problems. It would give her parents time to calm down, hopefully before marriage contracts were drawn up by Papa's solicitor, and more importantly, it would give the scandal the chance to die down, too.

And it would buy her freedom in a way that nothing else would.

She couldn't go alone, and she couldn't wait for her family to be ready to quit Halton.

But one person was leaving immediately.

And as far as Elodie was concerned, he owed her.

# Chapter Nine

"YOU'D BETTER HURRY. Sophia has sent word that Papa and the pig farmer are finishing up."

Elodie frowned at Hope while she frantically threw gowns and undergarments into a valise.

Hope had known Philip Harrison as long as Elodie had. She knew very well what the poor man's name was.

"I do hope Mr. Harrison will not be hurt by my actions," she said softly, wincing as Hope threw slippers and kid boots into the valise with gleeful abandon.

"Worry less about the farmer and more about the viscount, Elle," Cheska instructed, her blonde head appearing in the doorway. "If you don't manage to convince him to take you to London, then you're going to be dragged down the aisle kicking and screaming."

Before Elodie could respond, Cheska's eyes narrowed suddenly, and she turned her face away.

"That's Sophia's signal," she hissed. "Make haste, Elle. You're out of time."

Elodie stood rooted to the spot, a sudden misgiving washing over her.

"What am I doing?" she whispered. "I can't do this! I *don't* do this. This isn't me."

Panic clawed at her, closing her throat and making her heart pound uncomfortably.

Hope hurried over and snatched at the nightrail Elodie had been clutching, throwing it on top of the jumbled pile in Elodie's trunk.

Turning back toward Elodie, she reached out and took her sister's shaking hands in her own.

"Elle, listen to me," she whispered fiercely. "We all know that you have never done anything like this before. Heaven forbid Saint Elodie should put a toe out of line."

Elodie managed a scowl in the midst of her dread.

"But if you do not go now, you will be forced to marry or shipped off like some criminal. You've always been so concerned with doing what's right. But this? What's being done to you? It's not right, and you know it."

Elodie did know it.

But that didn't make this sudden and utterly scandalous rebellion any easier to stomach.

Thinking of Papa's anger and Mama's shame made Elodie feel like casting up her accounts.

But so did having to live under the same roof as her horrid uncle.

And though Philip Harrison was perfectly nice, she simply couldn't imagine herself tied to him for life. Having to see his cousin, Lord Brentford, at family events. Having to smile politely at him across a dining table, remembering his touch, his kiss—she just couldn't do it. Especially because he would marry, of course, and fill a nursery to carry on the viscountcy. And Elodie would be the poor relation married to the pig farmer.

It was prideful and downright idiotic. But she couldn't stomach the idea of it.

Besides, Philip *was* a good man, as she'd insisted to her scornful sisters. He deserved a better wife than a wanton hussy who would be lusting after his cousin over the roast pheasant at Christmastide.

"Elodie!

Hope's urgent tone brought an immediate cessation to Elodie's spiraling thoughts.

"Right," she said, albeit a little shakily. "I can do this. I can. I will."

The arrival of Cheska and Sophia set Hope and Elodie into motion.

While Hope and Sophia closed the valise and bulging trunk, Francesca reached out and pressed a reticule heavy with coins into Elodie's hand.

"Just in case your viscount doesn't help you."

Elodie frowned down at the velvet purse in her hands, a maelstrom of emotion battling for dominance in her thoughts.

What if Lord Brentford turned her away, and she had to go it alone?

Would that be better for her or worse?

Either way, her ruin would be complete the second she left this house.

The thoughts of being alone and using public transport to get to London put the fear of God into her.

The thoughts of being alone with the viscount cooped up in a darkened carriage for hours at a time made her perhaps even more afraid. Though for very different reasons.

Elodie was afraid of what might happen to her at the hands of ne'er-do-wells who lurked about the streets of London. And everywhere else, for that matter.

But she was deathly afraid of her attraction to the insouciant viscount and how he made her feel like throwing her principles clean out the window whenever she was in his vicinity.

The man couldn't have made it clearer that he had no interest in her. Yet here she was, about to sneak out of her home like a thief in the night to chase him down.

It was humiliating.

"This might not be such a good idea," she mumbled, balking once more at what she was about to do.

"Of course, it's a good idea!"

"Don't back out now, Elle. You're actually doing something

interesting for once."

"If you don't want to go after the viscount, I'll gladly take him off your hands."

Elodie scowled at all her sister's damning responses. Though Hope's quip about Lord Brentford stung more than the others.

"I *can't,*" she wailed, panic clawing at her throat. "Do you realize what this means for me? For all of you? If it got out that I wasn't in Bath and was, in fact, holed up in a carriage with a single man? Complete and utter ruin, that's what."

"If any of us were worried about that nonsense, we wouldn't be aiding your great escape, would we?" Hope huffed from atop Elodie's trunk.

Elodie watched as Sophia instructed Hope to bounce on the trunk while she fastened the clasp holding the bulging case together.

"How on earth am I going to manage that?" she asked, distracted from her ever-spiraling thoughts.

"You're not," Hope grinned. "Your viscount is."

"Right. That should do it," Sophia said as she straightened from the trunk. "It's going to take two of us to get this into the gig. Cheska, you grab that valise. Elodie, come on."

Elodie couldn't stifle a giggle, albeit a hysterical one, at Sophia ordering them all about.

*How would they even get away with this*, she wondered.

It wasn't odd to see the sisters out together, of course.

Elodie knew the residents of Halton thought of the Templeworth girls as endearingly madcap, excepting herself, of course, but this would be hard to explain away as youthful playfulness.

Still, it was too late to back out now. Not least because Hope and Sophia had already dragged her trunk out the door with Cheska following swiftly in their wake.

If she did stay, she'd have no clothes!

# Chapter Ten

CHRISTIAN SULKED IN the corner of the inn, brooding over a pint of ale that tasted a lot more watered down than usual.

This damned feeling of guilt was souring his mood. Coupled with the glares and scowls of the mad locals, it was enough to make a man downright angry.

And then, of course, there was the small matter of Miss Templeworth with her doe eyes and plump lips and the altogether tempting distraction she was.

He shouldn't have kissed her. Obviously. But nobody knew about it, and he didn't think she'd tell. It would hardly be in her best interests. Not if she wanted Philip to propose.

Unbidden, an image of Elodie married to his bland cousin popped into Christian's mind again, twisting his stomach in the oddest manner. He couldn't stop envisioning her, the picture of demureness, a quiet, biddable country wife. Her stomach round with his child.

Nobody would know the fire she kept so well hidden beneath the surface.

Nobody would know the passion that bubbled in her veins, just waiting for someone to draw it out of her.

He swore under his breath, irritated with himself for thinking that way. For caring.

The innkeeper's wife suddenly bustled past his table, ignoring him completely when he raised a hand to get her attention.

"That's it," he muttered under his breath. It was ridiculous for him to stay in this Godforsaken place a minute longer. He'd rather just pack up and go.

After watching Philip scuttle off to claim Elodie as a bride, Christian had sent for his driver and carriage immediately. The guilt he felt at cutting short the man's visit with family was just another thing to add to the ever-growing pile.

He'd sent Simmons ahead with the majority of his luggage and had intended to follow tomorrow on Ares, only keeping behind his personal carriage in case Ares came up lame. But he would just go now. When it got too dark, he'd find another inn to rest at. Hell, he'd bloody sleep under the carriage at this rate rather than put up with this for one more second.

Decision made, he tossed a couple of coins on the table and pushed back his rickety stool to stand.

A sudden cessation in the chatter around him drew Christian's attention, and he looked up to see the reason why.

A stunning blonde stood in the doorway of the inn, her crisp, lemon dress a stark contrast to the rough clothing and dark gowns of the people already inside.

He watched as she cast her gaze around the room, smirking as more than one man practically salivated over her.

Her brown eyes stopped on him, then narrowed, and he felt suddenly nervous.

She headed straight for him, marching through the busy room like a soldier on a mission.

And he suddenly realized who she was.

Elodie's sister. He couldn't remember which one. He didn't think she was the drunk.

And judging from the way she batted her lashes and took down every red-blooded man in the vicinity, she must be the flirt.

Christian didn't get it.

She was beautiful, of course. And she knew it, too.

But she didn't hold a candle to her softly lovely sister.

Was he the only one who saw that?

He thought suddenly of Philip and his obvious infatuation with the lady, and his mood turned darker still.

No, he obviously wasn't the only one.

The girl arrived at his table and, without asking permission, took a seat in front of him. He just managed to half-stand from his chair before she was seated, arms on the table, leaning forward and glaring at him.

"Miss Templeworth, isn't it?" he drawled, feigning disinterest. In truth, he was vastly curious as to what she was doing here, sitting uninvited at his table, glaring at him as though she'd like him to be wearing the tankard of ale that sat in front of him.

"Yes, it is," she responded drily. "I'm Hope. You remember Elodie, don't you? She's the woman whose life you've just ruined."

The little viper clearly didn't pull her punches. And he had a grudging respect for that. After his encounter with Elodie's parents that morning, he was glad to see that she had someone who cared for her happiness.

"I don't think that I ruined—"

"You're the cousin of the pig farmer, aren't you?" she continued as though he hadn't spoken.

He supressed a grin at her audacity.

"I am," he answered equably. "Mr. Harrison. I thought him well acquainted with your family."

Miss Templeworth rolled her eyes.

"We are as acquainted as I ever wish to be," she answered bluntly. "And now, thanks to you and your complete lack of honor, we'll be far more than acquainted. Forever. If he has his way."

Christian felt a spurt of anger at her aspersions. It wasn't because Philip had obviously done as he said he was going to and offered for the chit. Because that would be ridiculous.

But he'd never had his honor called into question so frankly. And if she had been a man, he'd have called her out for the insult.

"My honor? Miss Templeworth, I didn't—"

"Yes, yes. You didn't do anything wrong. Elle said as much." Christian blinked in surprise.

He had thought the beautiful Elodie would have been besmirching his name to anyone who would listen.

But it seemed that she'd defended him, even to her sisters.

There was that twist in his gut again. Guilt, yes. But something more. Something almost—tender.

Brutally, he pushed it aside.

"But neither did Elle," her sister was still speaking. "And she now has to pay the price for both of you. Either by marrying your cousin or being shipped off to Bath to be pawed at by our lecherous relations. Does that seem fair to you?"

Well, what was he to say to that?

Of course, it wasn't bloody well fair. But it also wasn't his problem.

He wasn't going to take on responsibility for the girl's father's idiocy or her mother's machinations.

No matter how good she felt in his arms. No matter that a sudden fury raged through him at the thought of her being pawed at.

But he didn't want to make the angry girl even angrier, so he stayed quiet and tried to stare her down.

He wasn't unaware of the stares they were getting, so she couldn't be either.

She, on the other hand, seemed marvelously unperturbed by them.

His staring down lasted all of five seconds before he felt the need to defend himself.

"I didn't do anything wrong." Christian knew he sounded like a petulant child. "Any more than El—than Miss Templeworth did."

At that, Hope rolled her eyes.

"Elodie never does anything wrong. Though I'd warrant that more than one person thinks being under a gentleman in the courtyard at night constitutes 'wrong.' Not me. I think it's positively marvelous. Especially with someone so delicious."

Christian couldn't help but grin at her scandalous words. And that smile was sheer devilment.

How did someone as angelic as Elodie Templeworth have such a hoyden for a sister? Come to that, how did she have *three* such sisters?

*But she's not so angelic, is she?* The thought came unbidden to his already busy mind. *Not when she's wrapped in your arms?*

Ignoring the blatantly flirtatious comment from Miss Hope, Christian got to his feet.

"Enjoyable as your company is, Miss Templeworth, I'm afraid I shall have to take my leave. I leave this evening. And much as I bear no will toward your sister, I am afraid that I have done all I can in explaining the real situation to your father."

The lady jumped to her feet, her eyes widening.

"You're leaving tonight?" she demanded.

"Er—yes?" He phrased it like a question because her behavior was suddenly as mad as every other person's in this place.

The sooner he got out of this damned insane asylum masquerading as a town, the better as far as he was concerned.

"Right now? Or later?"

*What is going on?* He wondered a little desperately.

She was mad.

"And will you return for your cousin's wedding to my sister?"

He hoped that he controlled his facial expression, even if he couldn't control the dark of jealousy at her question. "I am sure my business will keep me away," he answered hoarsely.

Her knowing grin set his teeth on edge. She looked as though he'd answered some secret question.

"Just so." She dimpled, suddenly looking cherubic. "Well, I shan't delay you any longer," she continued airily, and dipping a quick curtesy, she turned to leave in a flurry of skirts.

Christian noticed every pair of eyes in the room following her.

He couldn't figure this Hope chit out any more than he could her sister.

Still upset, he changed his mind about leaving right away and decided to eat before he left and would tell his servants to do the same.

# Chapter Eleven

"H OPE!"

They all turned to see Sophia running toward them.

"I'm going to need you to distract a footman or two, so we can sneak Elodie's things onto the viscount's carriage."

"Very well." Hope climbed back out of their conveyance, completely confident in her abilities to distract.

"Not just the bags," Cheska said as she, too, scrambled down to the ground. "Elle, as well. The viscount leaves very soon."

"W-what if he sees me and throws me out?" Elodie mumbled, feeling sick with nerves.

"He plans to ride his stallion, I'm sure of it. There is no way that a man of sense would allow someone else to ride a beauty like that," Sophia said.

"B-but—" Elodie tried to speak up, but she felt as though there was a boulder lodged in her throat.

"Although, how sensible can he be, really? If he's the cousin of the pig farmer?" Sophia continued contemplatively.

"I'm not sure if—"

"Hush, Elle. We don't have much time," Francesca scolded. "We need to ascertain if the viscount's valet will be traveling within the coach or if there's another for his luggage."

"I didn't see one," Sophia interjected. "Perhaps it went ahead?"

"Well, there's only one way to find out." Hope flicked an

errant curl over her shoulder and instructed Sophia to lead the way.

Francesca hurried after them, and Elodie, for lack of anything better to do with herself, brought up the rear.

This was utterly absurd, she knew.

If anyone saw them—a trail of Templeworths parading through the courtyard of an inn…

Well, she conceded even as she ran to keep up, nobody would be all that surprised, really. But they'd be shocked to see her involved, of that she could be sure.

"There."

Sophia's sudden stop meant that Hope crashed into her, Francesca crashed into Hope, and Elodie crashed into Francesca.

It added a level of ridiculousness to an already absurd situation. Especially because her sisters hissed and squabbled like toddlers as they tried to right themselves.

Hope disentangled herself from Sophia's and Cheska's limbs, heaving a deep breath and righting her skewed spencer.

"Right. Wait here."

They all watched as Hope glided toward three men eating close to a luxurious carriage emblazoned with the Brentford crest.

From where Elodie stood, she couldn't hear what Hope said.

But she saw them all notice her. Saw their eyes widen. And within moments, she saw the slightly dazed looks that gentlemen tended to get around Hope.

And because they were paying such rapt attention to Hope's face, they didn't see her signal behind her back, her hand curling to urge them forward.

"Excellent," Cheska exclaimed. "Let's get you inside."

"W-what?" Elodie blurted.

"Come on, Elle." Sophia began dragging her toward the carriage. "We need to get you inside the carriage. With any luck, the viscount will ride for a goodly time before he stops. So, if he drags you back, you'll have been with him all night. Even Philip Harrison wouldn't marry you after that!" she added triumphantly.

Elodie felt sick again.

"Oh, heavens," she murmured, rubbing at her throbbing temple. "I-I can't. This is madness."

"It's too late now," Cheska interjected firmly. "You've left a note at the house. If we don't get you into that carriage and out of this town immediately, you'll never escape."

Lord, but she wished she'd never started this, Elodie thought as she allowed herself to be dragged toward the black lacquered carriage.

Why had all of this seemed such a good idea at home? She'd panicked. That was the problem. Had she taken the time to calm down and think things through rationally, she would have come to her senses. She would have understood that a marriage to a good man, even one she did not love, was a perfectly pleasant life for a young lady.

Had she really thrown it all away in a fit? Just because she'd been kissed the way she had, by a man who'd clearly had an abundance of practice?

If she'd been alone, she would turn around and march right home to apologize profusely and do as her parents wished.

Instead, she'd dragged the three most reckless girls in England into this. And now they'd insist on her stowing away in his lordship's carriage. With or without her consent.

Well, she couldn't do it. It was as simple as that.

Digging the heels of her leather kid boots into the compacted dirt below her feet, Elodie forced the younger and smaller Sophia to a stop.

"Elle, hurry *up*," Sophia grunted as she tried to pull her along, but Elodie refused to budge.

"Sophia, stop," Elodie huffed.

How had her life become so chaotic in so short a time? How had one man turned her entire world upside down?

And it absolutely was because of that man. Of that, she was sure.

"We're not above kidnapping you, Elle." Cheska's tone brooked no argument. "We can do it the easy way or the hard way. But we *are* doing it."

The look in Cheska's blue eyes was as fearsome as the scowl on her face, and Elodie knew she had no hope of winning a battle of wills against her redoubtable sister.

The sisters continued on, coming closer to the back of his lordship's carriage. By now, they were within earshot of Hope's band of new admirers.

"So, the viscount expects you to hang about waiting for him whilst his valet gets to arrive in London hours before you? How grievously unfair."

If the men in Hope's thrall noticed her raised voice and clear attempt to have them hear everything, they didn't say anything about it.

Instead, they fell over themselves to assure her that his lordship had sent out their food with the instruction to be ready to leave as soon as they were done.

He was a wonderful master, they insisted. Kind and generous and fair.

Elodie didn't want to hear that about Lord Brentford.

She was already far too distracted by the memory of his superior features and passionate kiss.

She didn't need any more reasons to be infatuated with a man who would kiss her senseless and then leave without a backward glance.

And just like that, the spark of anger that had led her on this madcap adventure reignited, and she felt her resolve stiffen.

She wasn't going to meekly marry Philip Harrison and act as though he did her a great honor by taking on soiled goods.

And she certainly wasn't going to Bath to be treated abominably by her lecherous uncle and cousin.

This was not the time to be biddable. This was the time to take control of her own life. And if Lord Brentford could help her do that, albeit unwittingly, then so be it.

"Your trunk is already stored with the viscount's," Sophia whispered. "It was difficult, but I managed to squeeze it in. Here."

She ducked down and reached behind a carriage wheel, standing back up with Elodie's valise in hand.

"I couldn't fit this. And besides, I thought you'd need some of your things."

Elodie felt her eyes well with sudden tears.

She'd always felt just a tiny bit removed from her sisters.

But now, when she was the one in trouble, when she needed them, they rallied around her and took care of her.

It was nice, she realized, to be the one being looked after for once.

Sniffing, she reached out and took the bag from Sophia.

"Oh, for heaven's sake, don't start crying." Cheska's sharp voice brought Elodie's misty-eyed sentiment to an abrupt stop.

"Come. We'll open the door and get you inside. The viscount could come out here at any moment.

The sisters slipped to the side of the carriage, watching closely to ensure that Hope still had the servants' attention.

A quick sideways glance from her, a subtle nod as she dropped her reticule, sending the three men diving into the dirt for it.

"Hurry," Francesca whispered.

Sophia slid open the door of the carriage and gently shoved Elodie toward it.

"It's too high up," Elodie hissed. "I can't get in."

"We'll have to push you," Cheska said, and before Elodie quite knew what her sister was about, she'd grabbed hold of Elodie's bottom and started shoving her up and into the carriage.

The scuffle that ensued was nothing short of embarrassing, especially when Sophia joined in.

There were grunts and "ouches" and more choice words than Elodie would ever usually approve of, until finally, she landed skirts up, face down on the floor of Brentford's carriage.

"Did you 'ear that?"

Elodie, Francesca, and Sophia froze as one of the viscount's servants piped up.

"Hear what?" Hope thrilled. "I do hope it isn't a mouse or something. I should be frightened half to death. Perhaps I should walk back out to the courtyard, where there is better light."

Elodie rolled her eyes even as she stayed frozen in place.

It was incredible how easily led the male species were around a pretty pair of eyes and a head of golden curls.

The three of them stayed still until they heard Hope's voice fade away as she led her band of men in the opposite direction to the carriage.

When they deemed everything all right, Elodie righted herself and sat with a thump on the plush, velvet seat.

"You should lie down for a bit," Sophia said. "Make sure you're not seen yet."

"We'd better go, lest the viscount sees us hanging around his carriage," Cheska added.

There was a moment of complete silence as Elodie looked into the faces of her younger sisters.

Her actions today would have long-reaching consequences for all of them. Yet she knew they wouldn't want it any other way.

"Thank you," she whispered, a sudden lump in her throat. "Tell Hope thank you, too. And I shall see you all when you come to London.

"Take care and give that viscount for a fight." Cheska grinned.

"And ask him how much he paid for his horse, will you?" Sophia added with a grin.

A sharp whistle suddenly rent the air from the direction in which Hope had walked, and without another word, Francesca slammed the door of the carriage closed.

Elodie wished she could wave to her sisters, but she dared not try it.

She lay on the surprisingly comfortable cushioned seat, heart pounding almost out of her chest.

Listening intently, she couldn't decide whether she wanted to be caught or not.

Her heart skittered when she heard the viscount's voice, and, for one terrifying moment, she thought he meant to climb into the carriage.

But after what felt like eons, his voice drifted away, and suddenly the carriage was trundling out of the courtyard and onto the road to London.

She'd done it!

Elodie sat up, curling up in the corner of the bench. The small curtains on the window were open, but she was relatively sure that the dwindling light would mean that nobody would see her, should they look through the glass.

They were finally out of Halton.

She had run away.

There was no turning back now.

# Chapter Twelve

CHRISTIAN SCOWLED UP at the ominously dark rain clouds just as the first fat drop fell directly onto his face.

Riding through the rain was no trouble. He'd done it plenty of times before. But riding through the rain and the dark, with the road growing steadily muddier underfoot, was not his greatest idea.

Behind him, he heard the sound of the carriage trundling along, and he felt a pang of guilt, knowing that his driver and footmen were also getting soaked to the bone.

They were as used to it as he, of course. Probably more so.

But still, it remained unpleasant.

A crack of lightning illuminated the sky before him, followed by a deep rumble of thunder just overhead.

It was madness to continue like this.

He was far enough for the madcap town that he had sufficiently cooled his temper, enough to think clearly at any rate.

And as for the persistent, nagging guilt? Well, he'd ignore it, just like he'd been doing since he'd left Miss Templeworth's home.

Christian pulled on Ares's reins, bringing the beast to a halt, then turning him to meet the carriage.

"I think we need to stop," he told the driver. "If memory serves, we should be coming upon an inn in the next hour or so. Though it is late, I'm sure we'll be able to find a bed and some food for the night."

He noted the relief that flashed across the coachman's face.

"Very well, m'lord."

"Let me ride on, then." Christian had to shout over the lashing rain and thunder. As far as summer storms went, this one was a positive deluge. "I'll be faster on Ares. I'll secure myself a room and some quarters for you."

"Thank you, m'lord."

The driver and footmen doffed their caps, and without further ado, Christian turned Ares and traveled as fast as he dared in the direction of the inn.

By the time Christian arrived at the bustling inn, he was soaked through.

He eyed the number of coaches already in attendance, saw that the stables looked fit to burst, and began to worry that there'd be no room for him.

As soon as he stepped inside, he was hit with the raucous sound of chatter and laughter, the heat of the fire he could see blazing in a massive fireplace at the other end of the rustic but clean-looking room, and the smell of something delicious coming from what he assumed to be the kitchens.

His mouth watering, Christian removed his hat and futilely swiped at the drops clinging to his greatcoat.

Looking around for someone who looked as though they were in charge, he caught the eye of a rotund, ruddy-cheeked woman, who immediately battled her way through the throng and to his side.

"Welcome to the Horse and Carriage." Even whilst she smiled, she ran a knowledgeable glance over his clothing. "I am Mrs. Landry, my husband is the proprietor. Will you be needing a private dining room? They're in short supply due to the rain and it being so close to the Season. But I think we have a small one available."

She seemed to be awaiting his name.

"I am Viscount Brentford," he smiled. Running his gaze over

the packed room, Christian suddenly couldn't face the idea of the noise. Peace and quiet, space for his thoughts—that's what he wanted.

He felt like he hadn't had time to just sit and think since he'd come back to England.

"The small dining room should be perfect," he answered. "I've left my mount with a stable lad, and my carriage should be arriving momentarily. I'd appreciate a room for me and lodgings for my footmen and driver."

"You're in luck, my lord," Mrs. Landry beamed. "Our last available room happens to be our best. I'll send Mildred up to light the fire. If you'll just follow me? I'll see you into the dining room and send Mr. Landry out to your servants."

Her gaze searched the ever-louder crowd.

"Where is that blasted man?" she whispered, though it was loud enough for Christian to hear above the bustle.

"Oh, never mind. I'll see you to the dining room, my lord, it's the door right by the fireplace there, and then I'll attend to your servants myself."

Christian looked at the rain lashing against the windowpane.

He couldn't in good conscience allow a woman out in that.

"If you'll have a meal prepared for me, Mrs. Landry, and a bottle of claret, I'll go out myself."

The lady's eyes widened in horror.

"No, no, my lord. I couldn't—"

"I need to get something from my carriage," Christian interjected hurriedly. "Something of a—ah—personal nature. So I must insist on seeing to the men myself. If you'll tell me where to send them, I'll be back momentarily."

He could see the curiosity lighting the innkeeper's eyes and realized he'd need to bloody well retrieve something from his carriage now.

Perhaps he had lost a coin or watch fob or something behind a cushion. He could claim it held sentimental value for him. He certainly wouldn't be the first peer to have an eccentricity.

"There is a room just beyond the stables where the men can eat and bed down for the night," Mrs. Landry said. "The stablemaster can take care of your coach. If you're quite certain, my lord? I'm sure my husband will be out momentarily."

"I insist," Christian said firmly.

Without wanting to continue the somewhat odd conversation, Christian executed a quick bow and hurried back out into the pouring rain.

He spotted his crest on the side of one of the carriages and made his way over.

It took only seconds to relay Mrs. Landry's instructions to his soaking servants, who hurried off in search of a warm meal and somewhere dry to lay their heads.

Christian was rather looking forward to doing the same himself.

Hoping that he could find some kind of bauble or keepsake to satisfy Mrs. Landry's curiosity, he hurried around to the door of the carriage. Squinting against the teeming rain, he swung open the door and froze in complete and utter shock.

He'd wanted to find something inside the carriage—and he had.

For lying across the bench fast asleep, looking like an angel when she was obviously anything but, was Elodie Templeworth.

Christian stood frozen in place, rain pelting against his body, and simply stared.

What could he do about this? What the hell *should* he do about this?

More to the point, what in God's name was the chit doing stowing away in his carriage?

"Is everything well, my lord?"

Christian turned at the sound of his driver's concerned tone.

Damn and blast! What was he to do?

He turned back to look down at the sleeping woman in the carriage.

Frankly, he didn't know how to feel—angry that she'd put

him in this position certainly. Perhaps a little grudgingly impressed.

Should he take her straight home?

But how could he? They'd been driving through inclement weather in the dark for long enough.

Even Ares had been starting to feel the effects, flagging slightly beneath Christian's thighs.

He couldn't in good conscience drag any of them out in that again.

Besides, baffled and angry as he was, she'd been in there for hours. She was obviously tired, and she must be hungry.

An odd sort of protectiveness took him by surprise.

"Everything is fine," he answered without taking his eyes off Elodie. "You go on and enjoy your meal. I shall see you in the morning."

He heard the driver's goodnight. Heard the sound of his boots fading away. But still, he didn't move his eyes from her sleeping form.

So, when she suddenly stirred, her breath blowing a loose tendril of dark hair from her cheek, her eyes blinking rapidly and then moving to his, he saw them widen.

And amidst all the confusion and shock, he felt their impact like a punch to the gut.

# Chapter Thirteen

For a moment, Elodie thought she was still dreaming.

What else would account for the fact that Lord Brentford was still beside her, looking down at her?

Though, in her dream, he'd looked a lot happier to see her. And he was significantly drier.

Frowning slightly as he glared at her, reality started to slowly make itself known.

With a gasp, Elodie sat up and felt her hair tumbling down her back.

She must look a fright!

"M-my lord," she stammered, her head spinning, her stomach rumbling. "Are we in London?"

She would have thought it impossible, but his disapproving frown actually deepened.

"No, we're not in London, Miss Templeworth. But we're a long way from Halton."

"Oh," she whispered softly for want of anything else to say. "Where are we?"

He opened his mouth, and Elodie got the distinct impression he was about to shout at her. She stiffened her shoulders and prepared for the onslaught.

Might he throw her out on the side of the road, now that he'd discovered her? If he did, she didn't know what she would do.

But he didn't shout. Instead, he bit out a black oath under his breath and pinched the bridge of his nose.

She thought she heard some sort of prayer for patience before he finally looked back at her, his cobalt gaze boring into her.

"We are at a coaching inn, Miss Templeworth. A coaching inn where I have to stay the night." His pause felt ominous. "In the last room available."

Elodie gulped as the seriousness of his words sank in.

Of course, she'd known that they would have to take breaks on the journey. But if he had only been able to procure one room…

"I suppose you're rather curious about my presence here?" she offered, more to fill the awkward silence and to quiet her racing thoughts than because she had any real desire to explain herself.

If he returned her to Halton, her life would be over.

If he left her here, wherever here was, helpless and alone, her life would be over.

And though she wished that he were a good man, and his servants seemed to think he was, she didn't really know him. Certainly not enough to guess at what his actions would be. Especially because his face was granite-hard as he glared at her.

"You suppose correctly. I swear to God, I wish I'd never set foot in that damned village."

Elodie tried not to flinch, but his words stung.

She was tired and starving, overwhelmed, and terrified that she'd ruined her whole life.

And to her horror, she felt tears smart her eyes at his declaration.

For his own part, the viscount's eyes narrowed on her and then widened as though he were experiencing a similar horror.

"Are you *crying*?" he asked. Demanded, really.

"No," she sniffled.

A string of expletives, some of them rather impressively imaginative, rent the air before he snapped his mouth shut and glared at her once more.

"Right. Here's what's going to happen."

Elodie didn't particularly like his haughty tone but, considering she could still be left on the side of the road like a sack of rubbish, she thought it best to keep her mouth shut. At least for now.

"We're going inside where it's warm and dry. We are going to get you fed. And then you are going to give me some answers."

"Th-that sounds—reasonable," she said hesitantly.

"And then," he continued, the haughty tone and scowl still very much in place, "we are going to figure out how to get you home and how to get us both out of this mess you've made."

Elodie's hackles rose further still.

She wanted to point out that *he* had actually gotten them into this mess from the moment he'd followed her into the courtyard of the Assembly Rooms.

But it didn't seem the most opportune time to anger him further.

So, nodding meekly, even though she had absolutely no intention of returning to Halton, she stuffed her hair hastily under her straw bonnet, then gathered up her cloak and valise.

The viscount held out his hand, and Elodie eyed it, an inexplicable lump in her throat before she reached out and took it.

She tried to ignore the tingle that went through her fingers as his large hand gripped her own, and he helped her from the carriage.

Surely he would see reason.

There was no need for him to return her to Halton.

He was going to London; all he was doing was providing an escort, even if he hadn't known that until now.

What harm in an escort? Especially a secret one!

He would see sense. She would *make* him see sense.

In mere days they would arrive in Town, and he would never have to see her again if that was his choice.

Feeling more confident that this would all work out, Elodie tucked her hand into the crook of Lord Brentford's arm and let him lead her toward the bright lights of the inn.

"My lord, I thought you—oh!"

Christian gritted his teeth as Mrs. Landry drew to a halt, her eyes widening as they darted from him to the woman by his side.

This was exactly what he didn't want.

Already there was a speculative gleam in the redoubtable woman's stare. As someone who ran an inn on a busy London road, Christian could only imagine the things she'd seen. And she obviously assumed something nefarious was going on with Christian and Elodie.

It would serve Elodie Templeworth right if Christian were to allow the innkeeper and his wife to assume she was a lightskirt.

But even as he thought it, Christian knew he wouldn't tarnish the lady's reputation. And would, in fact, lie through his teeth to preserve it.

For that's exactly what he was about to do.

"I did tell you I'd left something precious in my carriage, did I not Mrs. Landry?"

Christian turned his most charming smile on the woman, pleased to see her cheeks redden and her eyelashes flutter.

"And nothing in the world is more precious than this lady. She had dozed off in the carriage, you see. We've had a rather tiring journey. My bride, the new Viscountess Brentford."

There was a moment of stunned silence, and he felt rather than saw Elodie Templeworth's huge, dark gaze boring into him.

But then Mrs. Landry squealed and clapped her hands together.

"Oh, my lord, my lady. Welcome, welcome. And felicitations to you both. Lady Brentford, I do hope you will find our modest dining room to your liking. If you would like a bath prepared, I can have a tub brought to your room whilst you dine."

Christian looked down at the diminutive girl by his side.

She was staring wide-eyed at Mrs. Landry, putting him in mind of a deer caught in a hunt.

Squeezing her hand gently, he smiled once more at Mrs. Landry.

"I'm afraid my wife is dead on her feet, Mrs. Landry, but I am sure she would greatly appreciate a bath."

The innkeeper's wife beamed at Christian.

"Let's get you settled into the dining room then, my lady," she said kindly.

Elodie still didn't make a sound as he gently tugged her to get her moving. She shuffled along beside him, seeming unaware of the gazes she was attracting.

But Christian wasn't unaware of them, and he wasn't bloody well happy about them either.

He doled out more than one warning scowl as they followed Mrs. Landry to the back of the room.

She opened the door to a small but clean and cozy dining room. The table in the middle was well worn but sturdy looking, and a welcoming fire was already roaring in the hearth.

"Now, if you'd like to settle yourselves, I'll bring through some food and wine. Unless you would prefer ale, my lord?"

"Wine would be excellent, thank you," Christian said politely, but his focus was still on Elodie.

He was soaked through, the rainwater seeming to sink into his skin. And he knew that he had been in the rain for hours longer than Elodie. But still, he worried that she'd catch cold.

He found himself wanting to fuss at her like a damned mother hen, so he strode toward the fireplace, removing his greatcoat as he went.

"Mrs. Landry?"

Both he and the woman turned at the sound of Elodie's timid voice.

"T-the bathtub. It will be sent to-to the viscount's chamber?"

Mrs. Landry darted a gaze between where Elodie stood looking tiny and vulnerable in the middle of the room and where

Christian stood brooding by the fireplace.

"Yes, my lady. Our last room but our best. I'm afraid that the rain has brought more travelers to our doors than usual."

There was another silence, and Christian felt his ire rise. He was cold, wet, hungry, and angry beyond belief.

So, to have to put on a charming smile for Mrs. Landry to reassure her that Elodie wasn't the victim of a kidnapping, which is how it would appear to anyone with eyes, was frustrating beyond belief.

Especially since she'd bloody well kidnapped herself!

Or something to that effect, at least.

"I know it is customary for ladies to have their own chambers, but—"

Gritting his teeth and preparing to act once again the charming, besotted groom, Christian stepped forward.

But to his surprise, it was Elodie who spoke up.

"Oh no, one chamber is perfectly acceptable, thank you."

Christian looked down at Elodie, noting the furious blush. And despite the farcical situation they were in, he couldn't control the slam of lust as he thought about them sharing a room—a room with one bed.

"I just didn't want to be apart from my h-husband for long."

Mrs. Landry's eyes misted over as she clasped her hands over her chest.

"How romantic," she sighed. "If I may be so bold, my lady, I could tell as soon as I saw you together that it was a love match between you. And such a handsome couple. I'm sure your children will be beautiful."

Once again, an awkward silence filled the air.

And once again, it was broken by Elodie.

"Thank you, Mrs. Landry. You are too kind."

The slightly interfering but well-meaning lady exited the room and left behind a deafening silence in her wake.

One that Christian had no idea how to break.

But Elodie surprised him again.

She turned to face him, her chin tipped upward, her eyes

huge pools that he could feel himself falling into, despite how much she'd angered him.

"I think that went rather well," she said airily. "Mrs. Landry seems to believe our story."

He could only stare at her, mouth agape.

This was her idea of a situation going "rather well"? The chit was as mad as everyone else in her Godforsaken village. And he was stuck with her.

"You and I have very different ideas of something going well, Miss Templeworth," he growled. "For my part, I don't particularly think there's anything remotely well about my being stuck with you, hours from Halton and days from London with no way to return you until tomorrow."

She flinched slightly at his words and damned if he didn't feel guilty, though he tried to push the emotion away.

He was in no way obliged to spare the feelings of the tearaway who'd put him in this situation.

"That was quite rude," she said piously, shocking him again with her audacity.

His guess was that her termagant sisters had had a hand in it all.

"But I'm sure once you've dried off and had a hot meal, you'll be less indecorous."

Christian's jaw was going to lock if it stayed open in shock much longer.

"And I'm sure once you've heard me out, you'll be much more amenable to helping me."

A pounding pain made itself known behind Christian's eyes.

"Helping you to do what, exactly?" he asked through gritted teeth.

Her smile was absolutely angelic. Now he knew the devilment that lurked inside her, he was less inclined to be taken in by it.

"To get to London," she said firmly. "I'm going to hide in Town until I figure out what to do with my life. And you're going to help me."

# Chapter Fourteen

ELODIE WAS RELIEVED at Mrs. Landry's fortuitous timing. For the lady bustled in with a tray laden down with bowls and cups followed by a maid carrying another, just when Lord Brentford looked ready to blister Elodie's ears.

She could only hope that what she'd said was true, and he'd be in a better mood when he was fed and dry from the rain. For she absolutely needed him on board with her plan now that he'd discovered her presence in his carriage.

She had been quaking in her boots when Mrs. Landry had mentioned them sharing a room, but she'd brazened it out.

Elodie smiled at the innkeeper's wife, determined not to draw any more unnecessary attention to their situation. It wouldn't do to make Mrs. Landry suspicious. If Papa came looking, and Mrs. Landry mentioned a viscount and his painfully uncomfortable bride, it would be obvious that it was she and Lord Brentford.

"This looks wonderful, Mrs. Landry," she said, drawing on all her years of deportment lessons to be the bland, society miss. "Thank you."

"Oh, you are too kind, my lady," the woman beamed. "Now, there is mutton stew, bread, cheese, some wine, and a pot of tea. I'm going to check on your bath and leave you to enjoy your meal in peace."

Within seconds, Mrs. Landry was back out the door, and Elodie once again found herself caught in the icy gaze of Lord

Brentford.

"Sh-should we eat?" she asked, trying and failing to sound nonchalant.

"Should we *eat?*"

Had he yelled, Elodie would have felt rather miffed. But his voice was low and deathly quiet and infinitely more intimidating because of it.

"Aren't you hungry?"

He stared at her, a scowl darkening his usually bright eyes.

"Miss Templeworth, have you completely taken leave of your senses?"

"No, I just—"

"You just endangered yourself. That's what you just did. Do you have any idea what might have befallen you if—"

"If what?" she asked when he drew to a sudden stop.

"If I were less than gentlemanly, Miss Templeworth."

Elodie could only imagine that she looked as skeptical as she felt, for his frown deepened further still.

"You do not agree that I have acted the gentleman?" he asked and seemed genuinely astounded. Perhaps a little hurt.

"Well, it's just that you aren't making this very easy or pleasant, frankly. And—"

"Easy?" he spluttered. "Pleasant? What would you have me do, Elodie? Fall to my knees and thank the gods that I have a runaway madwoman for company?"

"That's not very gentlemanlike," she chided and then wondered if someone's head might actually explode in anger, for the viscount looked as though that were a real possibility right now.

She listened, grudgingly impressed that he seemed to know so many curses in so many languages. At least, she assumed he was cursing based on the English ones that she understood and most certainly did not approve of.

Swearing in the company of a lady was *definitely* not gentlemanly, though it seemed prudent not to mention that at the moment.

After an age, he calmed. Throwing his head back and whispering what sounded like another prayer for patience, he finally leveled her once more with his ice-cold stare. "You have no idea the depths of ungentlemanly behavior to which men can sink, Miss Templeworth. If you did, you never would have taken such a foolish risk."

Elodie felt a shiver of fear at his words.

She wasn't quite so naïve as he seemed to think, but she was aware that she'd lived a rather sheltered life, too. Nevertheless, no matter what he thought of her sense and intelligence, she wouldn't have gotten into just anyone's carriage. She trusted the viscount. Ironically, given that she'd only ever had the wits kissed out of her by one man.

Some instinct told her that underneath the charm and rakishness, he was at least dependable. Perhaps not as honorable as she would have liked, considering he'd run away and left her to deal with the fall-out of their unfortunate courtyard interlude.

She was still hoping that she could salvage her reputation and family name after all of this.

Staying in London until the Season started in earnest was a sure-fire way to ensure that the gossip around her and Lord Brentford died down, that poor Philip would have the dignity of people not knowing that she'd run rather than accept a proposal, and keep her safe from uncles and cousins and anyone else who might paw at her.

All in all, she convinced herself—albeit a little feebly—this truly was the best course of action.

But she still needed this brute's cooperation.

Steeling herself to argue with whatever he was about to toss at her, Elodie lifted her eyes to clash with his own. But as she gazed into the depths of his glare, she couldn't quite seem to remember how to form an argument or even a coherent thought.

What was this—this *thing* that crackled between them every time she looked his way?

In some small part of her mind, she noted that as they stared at each other, his expression changed from angry to hungry, a sudden blue flame igniting in the depths of his eyes.

Without conscious thought, Elodie felt her body sway toward the heat of his.

And for a moment, she thought he would once again take her in his arms and kiss her.

The desire for him to do so took her by surprise.

This man, in only a few days, had made her question everything she'd ever known or thought about men. About life.

Closing her eyes, she prepared for what was sure to be a spectacular kiss. She tilted her chin, anticipation making her whole body tingle, and waited…and waited…

Nothing.

Frowning, she opened first one eye and then the other to see that he'd taken several steps away from her.

"Your food will be cold," he said stiffly, not a hint of the earlier heat present in his eyes or his tone. "Come. Eat. We'll discuss this rationally when you're better rested."

Had she so misread him? Was she so unattractive to him that he could coldly discuss Mrs. Landry's stew when she'd been ready to throw herself at him like some sort of lightskirt?

Tears stung at her eyes, but she refused, simply refused to let them fall.

Instead, she gathered the tatters of her dignity and glided toward the table where he held out a chair for her.

Steadfastly avoiding eye contact, she quickly removed her bonnet and cloak, draping them in front of the fire, then sat in the seat with a prim thank you, then proceeded to ignore him whilst she hastily re-did her hair with the dismal number of pins left hanging in her disheveled tresses.

It felt strangely intimate to be dressing her hair sitting across from him, even as she studiously avoided eye contact while she did so.

Though she'd been ravenous only an hour before, Elodie wasn't sure she'd be able to get a morsel of food past the lump in her throat. Still, she would have to eat something, especially since she still wasn't sure if she'd be dumped at the side of the road by the scowling viscount. And Mrs. Landry was so kind, the last thing Elodie wanted to do was insult the woman. So she ate in awkward silence, the only sound in the room coming from the fire crackling in the hearth.

Finally, after what felt like forever, a knock sounded on the dining room door heralding the arrival of a timid-looking maid. "The mistress sent me to tell you that your bath is ready, my lady. If you're finished dining. If not, there's no rush, the mistress said, and—"

Elodie jumped to her feet.

"I am," she blurted. "I am finished. I shall come directly."

Then, ignoring the viscount's brooding stare and the maid's startled look at her enthusiasm, Elodie darted from the room, feeling the viscount's eyes on her the entire way.

# Chapter Fifteen

CHRISTIAN RELEASED THE breath he wasn't even aware he'd been holding and got slowly to his feet. How was it that his life had been turned so dramatically upside down in only days by a woman who barely came up to his shoulder? A slip of a thing who shouldn't have any sort of hold over him, and yet somehow, frustratingly did.

God, when she'd been standing there gazing up at him with those incredible eyes, when he'd caught the scent of something floral and enticingly feminine, when she'd tilted her chin just so, as though she wanted him to kiss her as much as he did—it had taken the strength of Hercules himself to step away from her.

But this situation was stressful enough without letting lust addle either of their brains.

Despite his best efforts to remain furious, Christian couldn't help feeling grudging respect for the little spitfire.

And damned if those flashes of steely determination beneath such a quiet, timid demeanor didn't cause his blood to bubble with lust.

Mumbling an oath of frustration, Christian climbed to his feet and out into the main room, determined to drown his thoughts, sorrows, and headaches induced by the little termagant in ale.

And the most torturous part of the evening had yet to begin.

One room Mrs. Landry had said. One bedroom. With a bed.

*Damn it all.*

Christian stomped into the crowded bar and took up residence at a table in the corner. There didn't seem to be any sign of Mrs. Landry or the servant who'd come to take Elodie to her bath. Another expletive fell from his lips as he imagined her up there now, the steaming water surrounding her naked flesh. "Get a hold of yourself," he growled like a madman.

He hadn't been this tied in knots about a woman since the maid who'd taken his virginity as a lad.

Even then, he'd been in more control of his raging needs than he was right now.

"Good evenin', my lord. You look like you need a drink. Maybe even some company?"

Christian glanced up to see a serving girl gazing down at him with blatant invitation in her tired eyes.

He raked his eyes over her from the red curls haphazardly piled atop her head to the plump breasts shamelessly spilling from her gown.

Ordinarily, he might have enjoyed a harmless flirtation with the chit. Maybe even stolen a kiss if he got foxed enough. But tonight, his mind was too full of a dark-eyed innocent who kissed like a siren and was even now upstairs naked in the room they would be forced to share.

Christian gulped past a sudden lump in his throat.

This journey—should he agree to it—would kill him.

Could a man expire from unrequited lust? He had a feeling that he was close to finding out.

Smiling ruefully at the willing woman standing over him, he shook his head. "A bottle of your finest brandy," he said. The sting of rejection might slow down the procurement of the brandy he badly needed.

"And nothin' else?"

She was persistent, he'd give her that.

"A tumbler?" he responded with his most winning smile. "I don't think my *wife* would appreciate my swigging from the bottle."

At the mention of a wife, the chit straightened up, and with a shrug, she moved through the crowded room. Hopefully to get his brandy.

To his unending relief, she returned with a rather decent bottle and the requested tumbler, then, with nothing but a cheeky wink, she went on her way.

Christian suspected that she'd recover from his rejection quicker than lightning, and, sure enough, within minutes, she was happily perched atop the lap of another patron.

Pouring a generous amount of brandy into his glass, Christian downed the lot in one swallow before quickly pouring another.

This one he took his time over, staring into the amber liquid as he tried to think of what to do, and more importantly, tried *not* to think of Elodie upstairs and what she might be doing.

He couldn't return her to her madcap village. His guilt simply wouldn't allow him.

Because she was right.

He'd been happy to walk away, happy to leave Philip to clean up whatever mess occurred. Happy to ignore his attraction to her and even that odd jealousy he'd experienced imagining her with his quiet cousin.

So did he not then owe her this favor?

After all, what harm in just accompanying the girl?

The alternative was to dump her in her village, meaning he'd have to return, too, or leave her here stranded and alone. He immediately shied away from the latter thought, not even wanting to imagine what hands she could fall into. She had a steeliness in her that surprised him, given how demure she'd first seemed, and a feistiness that tempted him to the point of distraction. But she was still very much an innocent, of that he had no doubt, even if she kissed like a goddess.

It would only take one incident of her naivety to bring about her downfall. One bastard to do irreparable harm to her. The viciousness of his response to even the idea of a man putting his hands on Elodie took Christian by surprise.

She caused an odd protectiveness in him. One that was as unwelcome as it was unexpected.

Out of the corner of his eye, Christian saw that Mrs Landry was returning from upstairs carrying linens, followed by maids carrying stacked pots.

Elodie was finished her bath, then.

Much as he'd like to, Christian knew he couldn't sit down here in his cups forever.

He needed to go up there, talk to Elodie, and figure out how to get them both out of a potential mess.

And all the while, he told himself fiercely as he made his way up the wooden staircase toward the room, he would have to ignore the fact that he had her all alone tonight and probably for at least another week.

⇛⇚

NOW WAS NOT the time to panic, Elodie told herself as she combed through her hair by the fire. Unfortunately, her hair had always been heavy and thick, meaning it took forever to dry. 'Twas bad enough that she was in her nightrail and robe, but she knew she'd look insane to Mrs. Landry and the servants if she insisted on dressing after a bath.

But to have her hair loose and flowing down her back—what if the viscount took it as some sort of desperate seduction attempt?

What if he *welcomed* such an attempt?

Elodie ignored the wicked thought inside her head, just as she ignored her stomach's fluttering reaction to it.

She would never set out to seduce a man. Couldn't even if she tried, most likely.

She had neither Hope's penchant for flirtation nor Francesca's nonchalant disregard for rules. And even though Sophia was still young, she didn't have her little sister's confidence or sense of adventure either.

Elodie pulled at a particularly stubborn tangle in her hair, wincing at the pain.

Mrs. Landry had left a bottle of wine and two goblets on the small table by the fire, and Elodie hadn't missed the wistful smile on the kind lady's face as she'd wished her a pleasant evening.

She felt her cheeks heat as she imagined what Mrs. Landry had been thinking.

After all, if they *had* been newlyweds, surely Lord Brentford would want to—

A gentle knock on the door interrupted Elodie's sinful thoughts, and she jumped to her feet, her heart racing.

She'd been hoping against hope that her silly hair would have dried in time to put it up.

But she could hardly leave the man standing in the corridor! Not least because, he still hadn't agreed to help her.

Leaving a peer of the realm standing in a draughty hallway wasn't exactly proper behavior.

But neither was forcing him to be an unwitting kidnapper, to be fair.

The knock sounded again, a little louder.

There was nothing for it. She'd have to let him in.

She was trembling. Her heart was racing.

And there was a very real chance that she'd faint clean away. Preparing herself for his fury and hoping that her courage didn't fail her, Elodie walked slowly to the door and, taking a deep breath, pulled it open.

She watched as his eyes widened before perusing her from head to toe.

She didn't know what that look meant. She didn't know how to react to it. So she just stood there, staring while he stared right back.

# Chapter Sixteen

CHRISTIAN HADN'T KNOWN what to expect when Elodie opened the door. But he sure as hell hadn't expected her to look like the embodiment of temptation.

How was he supposed to survive a week of this?

He was well aware that he was staring but was incapable of tearing his eyes from her. The firelight from the hearth danced over her hair, which fell in delectable curls down her back.

Even more heart-stopping than those glorious curls, however, were the curves he could see now under the cotton nightrail and robe outlined by the light of the fire behind her. And he was to spend the night in here alone with her? If he managed to do so without putting his hands on her, he'd be in line to be sainted!

Christian swallowed past the sudden lump in his throat.

"M-Mrs. Landry left some wine," Elodie's voice was soft, and he heard the slight tremble in it.

She was probably worried about spending the night alone with him. And who could blame her? If she could hear his thoughts right now, she'd be running back to her safe, quiet existence forthwith.

"Kind of her," he answered, hearing the hoarseness of his voice yet unable to control it.

She didn't respond, and she didn't step back to let him in either.

Just stood there watching him with those heart-rending eyes.

"I-I don't know what to do," she suddenly blurted, and Christian felt his heart twist in the oddest manner at her frank vulnerability. "I've never been in this situation before."

Christian quirked a brow. "You mean you've never stowed away in the carriage of a man who's kissed you senseless, been discovered, and been forced to share a bedchamber with him?" he quipped. "I can't say that I have either."

Her lips lifted slightly at his attempt to lighten the too-serious mood.

Christian had been all set to march up here demanding answers and perhaps even insisting that she remove herself from his life.

But there was that guilt.

And those eyes...

"Perhaps we should try to discuss this calmly," he ventured now, trying and probably failing, to keep any trace of desire from his voice.

He was painfully conscious of the fact that they were alone in a room with one bed, so he could only imagine that she was, too.

"Alright," she agreed hesitantly before taking a deliberate step back and allowing him to enter the room.

Christian closed the door at his back and, for a moment, had to grip the handle to keep from reaching for her.

Damn, but she was exquisite. No wonder his cousin had been mad for the girl.

Though Philip had never seen her like this, Christian was sure.

She was, Christian realized with a start, the most beautiful thing he'd ever seen. And there she'd been, hidden away in a village of no consequence, living a pious, country life. Suddenly that didn't seem enough for her. She belonged in the best ballrooms adorned in the finest gowns and jewels. An image of her beside him at *ton* events, then beneath him on satin sheets, had Christian fighting the urge to pull at his suddenly too tight cravat.

*Christ!*

If he didn't get himself under control soon, he was liable to act on these feelings and scare the wits out of the lady.

Although, he remembered, she hadn't been scared the last time he'd held her. In fact, she'd been shockingly, seductively responsive…

"Lord Brentford?"

"What? Yes. What?"

He turned to see her looking at him like he'd run mad.

She had no idea how close he was to doing so.

Why, one night alone in her company would be enough to drive him to Bedlam, he was sure.

"I said that I am sorry for my state of dress. I—uh…" He watched, fascinated by the blush that stained her cheeks. "I thought it might seem odd if I were to dress after bathing, and I didn't want Mrs. Landry to—my lord?"

Once again, she was looking at him with consternation stamped across her face.

But really, what did she expect?

Bad enough that he'd been sitting downstairs imagining her in the bath. He could still smell the floral scent she must have washed with. And it was driving him insane.

But for her to then casually talk about her state of undress as though he weren't currently battling the overpowering need to undress her even more? It was too much to bear *and* have any sort of coherent conversation at the same time.

He was only human, damn it.

"Of course," he muttered hoarsely. "That-that makes sense."

Desperate to regain some equilibrium and distract himself from her—well, from her—Christian strode to the untouched wine and poured the deep, red claret into the two goblets.

He turned to hand one to Elodie, noting the slight tremble in her fingers as she took it from him.

And that one tell-tale sign was enough for Christian to get himself under control.

For much as he might want her, he wasn't a complete bastard, and he knew she must be terrified right now.

What he needed to do was get answers from her, get a plan in place, and then get the hell away from her and the temptation that swarmed between them.

Finally feeling a modicum of control, he gestured to the rustic wooden chairs placed on either side of the table. "Why don't we sit and talk this through?" he said, waiting for her to take a seat before taking the one opposite.

She eyed him speculatively, head tilted slightly.

Now what was going on in that head of hers?

"You seem—calmer than I expected," she suddenly confessed. "I thought that you meant to scold me. Perhaps drag me through the night back to Halton."

He answered her tiny smile with one of his own.

"Yes, well, I still haven't quite decided against that," he said flippantly. "So whatever explanation you give better be a good one," he finished with mock severity.

In all honesty, his severity should be totally sincere.

But she looked so nervous, so innocent, so lovely in the firelight.

And he knew then and there, no matter how this conversation went, he wouldn't return her to Halton and into the hands of his cousin.

Her smile widened, and Christian's idiotic heart squeezed in response.

Other parts of him were as affected by that smile, but if he let his thoughts wander down that road, frankly, he wouldn't be able to move away from this table for the entirety of their stay.

Miss Templeworth took a deep breath, flicking a strand of hair over her shoulder, and Christian knew that he'd find it nigh on impossible to concentrate on anything that came out of that delectable mouth.

"Mr. Harrison offered for me."

And just like that, as swiftly as his ardor had risen, it turned to ice.

Philip.

His cousin.

Shouldn't Christian feel bad for the man? Some sort of familial obligation to feel sympathy for his cousin's plight? Instead of this visceral jealousy?

And it wasn't as though the news was a surprise, in any case. He'd practically demanded that Philip offer for her.

But now that it had actually happened?

Well, he didn't like it. For reasons best left unexamined.

Taking a gulp of his claret, wishing more than anything that he'd brought the bottle of brandy upstairs with him, Christian let her words sink in.

Philip had offered for her, yet here she sat, across the table from him.

"You refused him?" he asked, his voice straining with the effort of keeping his relief from it.

"I…he…" She heaved another sigh. "I did," she mumbled miserably. "I am—quite aware of the compliment that your cousin paid to me by asking for my hand. But, but…"

Suddenly her eyes sparked with that fire he'd glimpsed before.

"He's a perfectly nice man, and I had no wish to hurt him. I just couldn't face rejecting him when he was so willing to suffer the gossip and the whispers."

Ignoring the now-familiar guilt churning his gut at the mention of the talk and whispers he'd left her to endure alone, he focused on the far more prominent feelings of confusion and horror.

"You mean you *accepted* him?" he demanded.

Elodie frowned across at him.

"What? Of course not! Why would I be sitting here with you if I'd accepted Philip's proposal?"

"An excellent question," Christian bit, stung by the impatience in her tone. "One I'd very much like an answer to, as you well know."

"I don't think it's fair that my life is decided for me because of something that didn't even happen," Elodie said miserably. "And I don't think it's fair that I should be forced into a marriage with a man whom I could never love because of it either."

"So you refused Philip?" Christian repeated, needing clarification with a desperation that he didn't exactly enjoy.

Elodie rolled her expressive eyes and whispered something under her breath that he couldn't hear but would stake his life on being insulting.

"I didn't refuse him, per se. I just—didn't exactly wait around for him to ask. Officially. He met with my father, and Cheska said they were discussing contracts and dowries, and I—well, I ran away."

"Wait," Christian said, leaning forward on his chair. "To be clear, you knew that Philip was going to offer for you, and instead of just refusing him, you ran away?"

Elodie scowled at him.

"You don't understand," she bit. "My father would have insisted. My mother would have cried and wailed. And poor Philip. He would have been crushed. My sisters would have suffered, too, had I refused him. Far better for everyone to have slipped away before he had the chance."

Christian could only stare at her, amazed at both her gumption and her fear of upsetting anyone.

Who was looking out for her?

Well, apparently, he was, as it turned out.

And the more they spoke, the less annoyed he was by that.

If anything, he was more determined to help her do whatever it was she felt she needed to do for herself.

"And nobody knows where you went?"

"My sisters know," she said.

Of course.

How could the three hoydens *not* be involved in such a scheme?

"And your parents? Where do they think you are? Or do they think you've disappeared forever?"

"Of course not," she said. "I left a note saying that I couldn't marry Philip, and I wouldn't be sent to my horrible uncle in Bath. But that I was safe, and I would see them in Town when they arrived for Hope's Come Out."

"And you think they'll just accept that, do you? Without trying to find you?"

"Perhaps not," she admitted grudgingly. "Not that it's any of your concern, but I said in my letter that they should tell everyone I'd gone to Bath like they threatened. I'm quite confident that Hope, Francesca, and Sophia will be able to stop them chasing after me. At least, they'll be able to delay them a while."

That scowl made a reappearance, and Christian found he quite liked it. It made her seem like an angry little kitten. He wanted to kiss the bad temper out of her so much that he clenched his hands to keep from reaching for her.

"At least long enough for me to get safely to London."

"Safely to London," he repeated. "And you decided I was the best way to make that happen?"

Surely that wasn't a burst of pride he was feeling. Surely he didn't care that she'd turned to him when she'd needed someone.

"Yes, I did," she answered stoutly. "For one thing, you owed me, considering you left me to pick up the pieces of our—ah—incident all by myself."

Christian winced as her barbed words hit their mark.

"And for another, well—I-I knew I could trust you to keep me safe."

This time her words hit him straight through the heart, and that fierce protectiveness she awoke in him reared its head. Along with another far more tender, far more dangerous emotion.

Elodie might feel safe with him, Christian mused as he watched the firelight dance across her lovely face.

But he suddenly felt far from safe with her.

# Chapter Seventeen

ELODIE HOPED SHE was doing a good job of convincing Lord Brentford to take her to London, but truth be told, her heart wasn't in the conversation, though her entire life hinged on his decision.

Truth be told, the only way she'd gotten through any of this was by imagining how Francesca would act and trying to mirror her formidable younger sibling.

For a moment, she'd considered acting as Hope would but had immediately shied away from the idea. Not least because it was far too tempting.

Hope would bat her lashes and flash her dimples, and frankly, Elodie wasn't convinced her own lashes were particularly battable. And she didn't have dimples.

But now, sitting in a silence that was surprisingly more comfortable than she would have imagined, she couldn't keep up the pretense.

She wasn't bold like Francesca. She didn't have it in her to demand his cooperation. Besides which, his eyes were so very blue in the firelight, and the lawn shirt she could see beneath his charcoal waistcoat was still damp from the rain, clinging to the muscles on—

"Miss Templeworth?"

Elodie snapped her gaze back to the viscount's, feeling her cheeks heat with the realization that she'd been sitting there ogling him like some sort of hussy, while he'd been trying to get her attention.

The smirk playing around his mouth didn't help to ease her embarrassment either.

"Was there something in particular that caught your attention?" he asked in an innocent tone that didn't fool her for a second.

Elodie felt her cheeks heat further still.

He was so ridiculously handsome. How was she supposed to keep her wits about her?

"Your shirt," she blurted before her brain could control her silly mouth.

He raised his brows, the smirk growing wider still.

"My shirt," he repeated, and the glint in his eyes was so wicked that Elodie's breath caught.

Oh, dear. This would absolutely not do. She couldn't allow herself to feel anything for such a cad. She couldn't allow herself to imagine him reaching for her, pulling her close to that dampened skin, and picking up where he'd left off in the hallway of her house.

What on earth was wrong with her? She'd never felt so wanton, not once in her life. Yet around Lord Brentford…

"I merely worried that you hadn't yet had a chance to dry off, my lord. Y-your shirt still appears to be damp. And I thought that perhaps it might be p-prudent if you were to undress. I mean dress. I mean…"

There was nothing for it. Her embarrassment had tied her tongue completely, and she stumbled to a halt, heart racing and mouth dry as a desert.

The silence fairly crackled between them, and Elodie didn't know how to break it. Trying to channel one of her indomitable sisters was no use. Trying to remind herself how serious this situation was did nothing.

Nothing could distract her from the way he made her feel.

The tension was suddenly unbearable, and Elodie jumped to

her feet, knocking her chair over with a loud thud.

"I-I'll leave you to change then, my lord," she mumbled, eyes fixed on the floor as she hurried by him.

She made it less than three steps before he was standing, his hand reaching out to grasp her arm.

"You can't go out in your nightclothes, Elodie," he said, and her heart thumped painfully at the sound of her name on his lips.

She should scold him, of course. She hadn't given him leave to use it.

But she stayed quiet, her eyes slowly lifting to meet his own.

"I could just step outside the room," she said, hating the tremor in her voice but unable to do anything about it.

His lips quirked.

"That's very chivalrous," he quipped, "but quite unnecessary. I wouldn't have you standing in a darkened corridor alone."

"But-but I cannot stay in here while you, well, while you…"

"Undress?" he offered helpfully.

Elodie gritted her teeth, sure that he was enjoying her discomfort.

"Quite," she sniffed, earning herself a full-blown grin.

"You can turn your back in deference to my modesty," he offered. "And no peeking."

Elodie's jaw dropped at his audacity.

"One can't be too careful with one's virtue, Miss Templeworth," he said piously, though his eyes glittered with wicked humor. "And you've already admitted to gawking at my chest, so—"

Elodie gasped. "You odious, arrogant—" She smiled.

"Come now, my dear. If we are to be traveling companions to Town, don't you think there should be honesty between us if nothing else?"

"T-traveling companions? You mean you will take me to London?"

She couldn't keep from beaming up at him. She felt giddy with relief that he wasn't going to abandon her or force her to return to Halton. And in a move that was completely spontaneous and alien to her, she reached up and flung her arms around his neck. "Thank you, my lord."

Elodie felt him stiffen and was immediately ashamed of her rash behavior.

She pulled her arms behind her back and took a very deliberate step back.

"My apologies, Lord Brentford," she addressed her words to his muddy Hessians, refusing to meet his gaze. "I-I'll leave you to get dressed."

Before she had the chance to turn away, his hand came to cup her face, tilting her chin and forcing her to meet his eyes.

What she saw in their blue depths made her forget any thought of embarrassment, any thought of London or Halton or anything else.

And before she could guess at his intentions, his mouth rushed toward her, and all she could do was cling to him as he set her world on fire.

⟫⟫⟫✕⟪⟪⟪

CHRISTIAN KNEW THAT he should keep his distance from the alluring Elodie.

But hell, having her throw her arms around him was more temptation than he could fight.

The second his lips descended on her own, the second he felt her capitulation, he was lost.

Never before had he lost control so completely, so quickly.

Her body was soft and pliant, molded to his own in a way that sent lust coursing through his veins.

He had a brief moment of sense, where he thought he'd have the strength to move away from her.

But then she sighed, and the breathless sound sealed both their fates.

With an oath of surrender muffled against her lips, Christian pulled her closer still and delved his tongue inside her mouth.

It wasn't enough: the feel of her own tongue dancing with his, the press of her breasts against his chest, her hips pressed against his. He needed her closer. Needed more of her.

A sort of madness was taking over him, dulling everything except the feel of her, the scent of her, the taste of her. He moved them, walking her backward until her back hit the wall, and he could press himself closer still, his groan mingling with her breathless moans. With one hand cupping the nape of her neck, her silken tresses falling over it like a waterfall, he moved the other to explore the scorching curves and contours of her body.

Her simple cotton nightgown offered almost unhindered access to her body, and he thanked every deity he could think of that he didn't have chemises or stays or stupid little buttons and frills to contend with.

Wrenching his lips from her own, he trailed his tongue along the smooth column of her neck, stopping to bite gently at the wildly fluttering pulse beneath her ear.

She writhed beneath his ministrations, and Christian felt the last vestiges of his control start to fray.

He knew that he couldn't take her here and now. Of course he did.

But damn it, he'd never been pushed so close to the edge so quickly.

His hand dipped inside the loose neckline of her nightgown and found one soft, full breast, and he almost expired from want when she thrust boldly against his fingers, when he wrenched a desperate whimper from her lips as he flicked his thumb over the hardening nipple. Moving his lips from her neck, he returned to her mouth, capturing the sounds and swallowing them greedily.

They were past the point of sense by now, he knew.

He pulled at her skirts, growling in response to the feel of her silken thigh beneath his knuckles. He felt like a caged animal about to break its chains and devour its prey.

His focus was all on her now, his mind entirely on the pleasure he was about to give to her, to them both.

And nothing would stop him. Not morals, not Philip, not her innocence, or his conscience.

"Please, Christian," she whispered against his lips. "Please."

Christian knew that she had no idea what she was asking for, but he sure as hell did. And he intended to give it to her, consequences be damned.

His searching fingers finally found the center of her, and he took her mouth more urgently now as he moved toward it.

The anticipation, the pleasure was almost painful in its intensity. Losing patience, he hitched her thigh, so her leg was wrapped around his own, allowing him the space he needed to finally—

A sudden knock on the door beside them sounded, and Christian sprang away from her as though he'd been burned. He looked at her, watching her eyes widen as the haze of desire left them.

She pushed away from the wall, pulling at her gown and tightening the belt on her robe that had come undone.

Not once did she look at him. Not once did she speak.

And Christian didn't either, for he had no idea what to say.

The knock sounded again, a little more urgently this time, and he cursed whomever it was to perdition as he marched to the door, watching her stagger toward the chair he'd occupied before throwing her head into her hands.

Christian threw open the door, prepared to blister the ears of whatever maid had interrupted them or thank her profusely. He couldn't yet think straight enough to decide which.

He glowered at the serving girl, who gawked at his furious expression before holding out a jug of water to him.

"Mrs. Landry thought you might want fresh water to clean up with, my lord," she said a little warily.

And who could blame her?

Christian could only imagine he looked like a beast since he felt like one right then.

Smoothing his expression as best he could, he offered the girl his most charming smile.

"Thank you," he said. "Tell Mrs. Landry it is most welcome."

The maid bobbed a curtsey before rushing off down the hall-way.

A part of him wished quite desperately to run off after her and get as far away from Elodie Templeworth as he could.

Instead, he shut the door, the click sounding more ominous than it should.

Then, without knowing what on earth he would even say, he turned to face her.

# Chapter Eighteen

ELODIE COULDN'T STOP shaking.

No matter what she did, what she said to herself, her entire body was trembling.

And her brain was currently the consistency of porridge.

What had they done?

What had *she* done?

How had she, in the space of mere days, become someone who would kiss a man like that? A virtual stranger, no less. And what's more, be begging him for more!

Hope would be delighted. Francesca, probably impressed. Only Sophia would be suitably disgusted. Not because of Elodie's awful behavior, but because she was twelve and not yet interested in the opposite sex.

She heard Lord Brentford open the door, heard his brief conversation with whoever had unwittingly saved her from herself.

Because it wasn't the viscount's fault, Elodie had to admit. She'd been as willing as he, as enthusiastic. More so, actually, since only one of them had been begging shamelessly, and it hadn't been him.

Elodie felt tears of confusion and shame smart her eyes.

She was tired; that was all. It had been a fraught and exhausting couple of days.

Besides, once they got to London, she'd never see Lord Brentford again.

Ignoring the foolish stab of pain she felt at the thought, Elodie spun to look out the small window overlooking the still-bustling stable yard.

She heard the sound of the door shutting but didn't turn around. Couldn't turn around. Her emotions had her locked in place as though she'd grown roots.

The silence stretched painfully as she waited to see if he would speak to her, what he would say.

But after eons, he merely sighed.

Holding herself rigidly still, she listened to the rustling sound of clothing being removed, swallowing a lump in her throat as she imagined his movements.

The splash of water told her that he was washing and, wanton as she now apparently was, she couldn't help but wonder if he'd removed those damp clothes whilst freshening up.

After what felt like hours, he spoke.

"You're not going to sleep standing up, are you?"

Though his voice was light and teasing, she sensed the undertone of something darker lurking beneath it and, Lord save her, but she reacted to it immediately.

She had to face him, she knew that, and yet she could not seem to get her body to turn around.

What if he looked at her with disgust? What if he refused to take her to London now because of her indecorous behavior?

Or worst of all, what if he assumed that she would allow him to…to…

She couldn't even think it without feeling sick.

Well, there was only one way to find out, she supposed.

Elodie straightened her shoulders and turned to face him.

She couldn't help but think of what Hope or Cheska would say.

Hope would probably laugh it off as nothing serious.

Cheska would insist that if Elodie were indecorous, then he was just as bad.

But her sister didn't understand that things were different for ladies. Or rather, didn't care that they were supposed to be.

Her breath hitched once more as she took in his appearance. To her relief, he was dressed, or partly so in any case.

He stood barefooted before her, his black breeches hugging the legs that she knew were rock hard.

But it was his torso that caught her attention the most. He wore only a lawn shirt, untied and free from a cravat.

The open ties gave her the barest glimpse of his throat, and further down, his chest. The material was light enough that she could see the outline of his broad shoulders, the rigid muscle of his abdomen. He was like a work of art. A sculpture come to life.

And she'd had that—all of that—pressed against her only moments before.

"I'm afraid that this is the best I can do," he said, and if she didn't know how arrogant he was, she'd think he appeared rather self-conscious. "I wasn't exactly expecting company this evening."

The boyish grin was almost her undoing, but Elodie managed to hang on to her rigid demeanor.

"My lord," she sounded as stilted and banal as she had when they'd first met, but if that's what it took to get through this excruciating evening, then so be it. "I wanted to assure you that I am not the type of person to, to…"

Gads, but this was embarrassing.

"What we did—I don't wish for you to have the wrong sort of impression of me." It felt nigh impossible to hold his gaze while she forced the words out but she did so, needing to see that he believed her, needing to see that he understood.

He was silent, watching her contemplatively from across the room. "Elodie," his voice was gentle, his steps slow as he moved toward her. "I could never think you anything other than exactly what you are."

She frowned in confusion at his cryptic remark.

It didn't *sound* like an insult, but she had no idea what he meant.

His grin set her poor overworked heart fluttering again.

"And what you are is a brave, beautiful, slightly insane, but utterly charming lady."

Well, that was rather nice. If one discounted the insane part.

"My impression of you is that though you are outwardly saintly, you are made for sin, Elodie Templeworth. And I'm beyond grateful to be the man that got to discover that."

Elodie could only watch him as he came closer still.

"But there is no doubt as to your excellent character. Mine, however, leaves a lot to be desired. Because there's not a single part of me that can bring myself to regret what just happened."

Elodie didn't know what to say to such a thing. Didn't particularly know how to feel about it either, truth be told.

She was rather thrilled about it but knew that she shouldn't be, of course.

He was only inches from her now, and she could smell the soap he'd obviously used whilst washing. He smelled clean and masculine and devastatingly tempting.

"You have no cause to worry about my opinion of you," he said softly. "But I'm a base enough creature to admit that I don't think us sharing a bedchamber is the most prudent of ideas. There's only so much torture a man can take."

His boyish smile was completely disarming.

"But Mrs. Landry said there were no other rooms," she said, wondering if he could hear the breathlessness of her tone.

"Not to worry," he said. "I find myself in need of something stronger than wine, and then I think I shall bed down elsewhere. Perhaps in my carriage. You seemed to manage to sleep rather well in it."

Elodie felt a pang of guilt at the idea of him folding his large body onto the tiny bench.

She couldn't in good conscience commandeer the man's bed after forcing him to stow her away to London.

He must be over six feet tall. It would be far easier for her five feet and four inches to fit in the carriage.

"Lord Brentford, please. I can't take your bed from you. I am smaller than you are. I'm sure I could—"

"No."

His refusal was abrupt, his tone brooking no argument.

And Elodie's ire rose at his high-handedness, even though she knew it shouldn't.

"What do you mean, no?" she demanded, all shyness forgotten as her temper flared. "You won't fit in the carriage."

"And I won't let a lady sleep alone in a carriage in the stables of an inn," he shot back. "How could you even think that I would?"

She didn't think that, to be fair.

Contrary to what she'd accused him of earlier, aside from turning her world upside down with his kisses, he was quite the gentleman. And he had agreed to continue her kidnapping, which was very kind, all things considered.

Elodie huffed out a breath and cast her gaze around the room.

There really weren't any options.

"I could take the counterpane," she offered hesitantly, "and sleep in front of the fire?"

He quirked an arrogant brow.

"Nor will I allow a lady to sleep on the floor," he muttered through clenched teeth. "Honestly, Elodie—what do you take me for?"

She threw her hands up.

"Well, what are we to do then?" she asked, suddenly thoroughly fed up. "Because Mrs. Landry can't see you sleep in the stables. Not if we're to keep up the pretense."

He glared at her for a moment, and then, in lieu of answering, he strode to the bed and pulled the counterpane from the bottom, then snatched up one of the pillows.

"Get into bed, Elodie," he said in that haughty tone once more. "We'll be setting off early in the morning."

"But what are you doing?" She frowned.

"I am making myself as comfortable as possible, and then I'm going to sleep."

She watched in consternation as he dragged her overturned chair in front of his own, then sat in one, putting his feet on the other, then leaned his head back against the rickety wood of his chair.

Elodie didn't know what to say or do as she watched him throw the counterpane over himself.

He wouldn't be able to sleep like that, she knew, and her guilt reared its head again.

"I'm smaller than you," she pointed out mutinously. "Surely it would be more sensible for me to—"

His long-suffering sigh interrupted her, and his head snapped up, ensnaring her in his ice-blue stare.

"You are the most frustrating woman I've ever met," he bit out. "I am not letting you sleep outside. And I am not letting you sleep on a chair. Therefore, you will take the bed. I will take the chair. Mrs. Landry will be none the wiser. Now, it's been a long and absolutely mad day. So get some sleep."

Feeling well and truly chastised, Elodie decided not to argue further.

Wordlessly, she moved to the bed and dove under the covers.

The moonlight shone through the window, the fire crackled merrily in the hearth, though she could hear that it was beginning to die down, and Elodie tried to relax as best she could. But she was painfully aware of his presence just feet from where she lay.

The silence stretched on, and she wondered if he'd fallen asleep.

Despite the tumultuous emotions raging inside her, Elodie felt the day's events weigh heavily on her body, and to her surprise, her eyelids began to droop.

Right before she drifted off to sleep, his voice sounded in the darkness.

"Goodnight, Elodie."

Her heart flipped at the simple words.

"Goodnight, my lord," she answered a little croakily.

"Haven't we gone beyond the need for 'my lord'?"

She couldn't see his face, but she could hear the teasing in his tone.

And although they had crossed the bounds of propriety far too many times in far too many ways, she found herself smiling.

"Goodnight," she repeated softly. "Christian."

He didn't answer, and Elodie drifted off to sleep listening to the deep, steady rhythm of his breathing.

# Chapter Nineteen

"I T DOESN'T LOOK like the storm plans to let up, my lord. You might be as well to ride inside the carriage this morning."

Christian gritted his teeth as he imagined Elodie's reaction to being in close quarters with him.

He gritted his teeth imagining his being so close to her.

Last night had been agonizing enough.

He hadn't slept, which wasn't surprising given that he'd spent the night with his arse planted on the most uncomfortable piece of furniture in Christendom.

It wasn't the chair that had kept him up, though. At least, not only the chair.

In truth, he had spent half the night driving himself mad remembering every detail of his explosive kiss with the impertinent miss in the bed across from him, and then the rest of the night being driven mad by her soft sighs, by every movement he could hear when she turned over.

He knew that the pillows would smell of the flowers that seemed embedded in her skin. Knew that the sheets would be warmed by the heat of her body. And when he'd eventually managed to doze off, his dreams had been so filled with images of her in that bed that he'd woken in a cold sweat.

"My lord?"

Christian snapped back to the present at his driver's voice.

"Er—yes," he said, trying to remember what they'd been

talking about. "We'll be ready to leave after we've broken our fast then."

"We?"

Damn it all.

Christian had quite forgotten that his driver and footmen had no idea that they'd been dragged into the tormenting Templeworth girls' plan.

"Er, yes," he tried thinking on his feet but after a night of no sleep and the prospect of days and nights alone with Miss Elodie, he found thinking quite the challenge. "My…um…my wife. My new wife, that is. She…I…"

He rubbed the back of his neck, squirming under his driver's astonished gaze.

It wasn't as though he owed his servants an explanation.

But then, servants gossiped more than Society biddies, and he had Elodie's reputation to think of.

Although, it would be beyond strange when word flew around Town of his non-existent marriage.

Clearly, he wasn't very good at this.

"That is to say, my future wife," he scrambled for a modicum of sense. "I am recently betrothed, and my fiancée is traveling to London with me ahead of her family. To-to purchase a wedding gown."

What on earth was he saying?

It seemed the Templeworth madness was catching.

"And she… Her father entrusted her to my care just this morning so—so we will both be ready to travel within the hour."

"Er…very well, my lord."

Christian gave a brief nod to his baffled-looking driver before turning swiftly and heading back toward the inn.

He'd requested a breakfast tray from the misty-eyed Mrs. Landry, claiming that his bride and he wanted privacy.

He absolutely *didn't* want privacy with Elodie. Perhaps less so now that he'd have to confess that they were betrothed should his servants inquire.

She'd weaved quite the web, and he was getting ever more ensnared in it.

He wondered, not for the first time, if he'd made a mistake agreeing to this entire thing.

But then he'd remember that smile, that hair, those glorious eyes, and he knew that he'd find it hard to refuse her anything.

Even the simple pleasure of hearing his name on her lips, whispered into the still night, was more than he'd experienced in a long time.

Unbidden, he thought of Cressida, whom he hadn't seen in over a year since his business interests had taken him overseas.

Before that fateful dance with Elodie, he'd been looking forward to a reunion with the red-haired beauty.

But now…

*No, Christian,* he told himself sternly as he darted inside out of the torrential rain. *You can't let a couple of days and two kisses change the entire course of your life. You'll get her to London, then you'll get the hell out of her life.*

Why did that idea sit so uncomfortably with him?

Frustrated with his uneasy thoughts, Christian spotted Mrs. Landry heading up the staircase carrying a tray laden with refreshments and hurried to intercept her.

"My dear Mrs. Landry, might I assist you?" he asked, all charm and chivalry, hoping that the tray was intended for him and Elodie.

"Oh, good morning, my lord," Mrs. Landry beamed at him as he reached out to pluck the heavy tray from her hands. "As it happens, I was just taking the tray to the viscountess."

Christian's heart did the oddest little flip as the older woman referred to Elodie as his viscountess.

But he couldn't even begin to wonder at its cause with so much already fascinating him about the lady, so he merely smiled his thanks and insisted that he take the tray upstairs himself.

After profusely thanking him, Mrs. Landry bustled off back down the stairs, and Christian prepared himself to face the torment of seeing Elodie again and trying to keep his hands off her.

The door to their bedchamber was shut, of course. And he didn't know quite how to knock politely with a tray of breakfast things in his hands.

Hoping that she still slept, Christian bent down and, with some difficulty, managed to open the door with his elbow.

He stepped quietly inside, listening for any sounds of Elodie moving about. But there was only silence.

Closing the door as gently as possible behind him, he set the tray down on the table beside the fireplace. This morning he'd been awake early enough to inform the scullery maid that they wouldn't need the fire.

But now—

He crept closer to the bed, and there she was, sleeping like an angel.

Christian felt his heart flip again as he took in the sight before him.

Though it was dull and grey outside, somehow, she managed to look bathed in light.

Her cheeks were flushed, one of them resting atop the hand she'd tucked under it, and her hair sprang in disarray on the snow-white pillow.

She looked innocent, fragile. Beautiful and pure. And all the more desirable for it.

A sudden panic took hold of him as he stood there watching her sleep. It was becoming far too easy to fall under her spell. Far too easy to forget the path he'd set for himself. He'd run from Halton to avoid the situation that he was now in danger of running toward.

And it needed to stop.

Dragging himself under control, he leaned down and stroked his knuckles along her satin-smooth cheek.

It didn't need to stop right *now*.

He watched, mesmerized by the fluttering of her lashes as she came slowly awake.

Her eyes opened, blinking once, twice before settling on him. He felt their impact right down to his toes. And then she smiled at him—a slow, sensuous expression that made his entire body heat with longing.

"Time to get up, lay-a-bed," he said gently, trying his hardest not to imagine them waking together every morning. "We leave for London within in the hour."

She frowned up at him for a moment before her expression cleared, and she bolted upright.

"What time is it?" she asked, rubbing her eyes.

"Don't worry, 'tis early yet," he said. "Come, break your fast with me. The weather hasn't improved any, I'm afraid to say. But the carriage should be comfortable enough."

"Did you sleep well?" she asked as she pulled on her robe before climbing from the bed.

Christian averted his eyes, lest he tumble her back onto the mattress and finish what he'd started last night.

"Ah, yes. Some," he lied, standing by his seat until she took hers.

"I should dress before we eat," she said quietly, her cheeks pink.

"I won't tell if you don't," he winked, delighting in her soft laugh.

"You've quite made me forget myself, my lord," she quipped but seemed happy enough to stay as she was as she began pouring tea and lifting covers off plates and bowls.

"Are we back to 'my lord' then?" he asked as she passed him a cup and saucer.

Tea.

He despised the stuff.

But he took it, nonetheless.

"It is more proper."

"And here I've been calling you by your given name without any thought to propriety."

She grinned up at him.

"I won't tell if you don't," she said, and Christian couldn't contain his laugh.

He found himself suddenly desperately glad that she hadn't tied herself to one such as Philip.

Though he felt some sympathy for his smitten cousin, it would have been a crime for her to have hidden all that wit and vivacity on a farm in the countryside.

"Very well," he nodded. "We shall both keep our secrets."

"We make quite the pair, don't we?" she said.

Christian gazed at her, falling further under her spell. "Yes," he answered, an odd tremor in his voice. "We do."

# Chapter Twenty

ELODIE'S HEAD WAS pounding, her shoulders stiff and sore as she sat in the carriage and watched the viscount sleep.

Her shock that morning when he'd told her that they must fake an engagement between them in front of his servants was immediately put from her mind when she realized he intended to travel inside the coach with her.

She shouldn't have been surprised, not when the rain showed no sign of abating.

But that didn't stop her nerves from being fraught for the entire journey.

Mrs. Landry had packed them off with a basket of food and it sat at their feet now untouched.

Christian had made polite, airy conversation for the first hour or so of their journey. But he'd soon quietened and then fallen asleep, his head against the plush velvet cushion, his legs stretched out in front of him.

She suspected that he'd lied about sleeping last night, and so touched was she at his chivalry that she happily allowed him to sleep away the hours of their journey.

And it was a relief, in any case, to have time to herself. To let her eyes wander over him without fear of being caught. To let her mind wander unchecked down paths she knew it shouldn't be going.

But she couldn't relax. His proximity was excruciating.

Not even the humiliation she'd felt last night was enough to stop her from wanting a reoccurrence.

She would have to spend weeks if not months repenting for such sinful thoughts, yet she could not entirely regret them.

For her whole life, she'd assumed that of all the Templeworth girls, she was boring, bland, and dull.

But the feelings Lord Brentford invoked in her were quite the opposite.

And though they were futile, it was quite nice to know she was capable of passion.

She sighed and looked out the window.

Perhaps a book might help her while away the hours until they stopped for luncheon.

However, not even the gothic novel she'd stolen from Hope was enough to hold her attention.

And the writings of Mary Wollstonecraft that Cheska had insisted she pack required far too much attention than she was capable of giving at the moment.

So, no reading then.

She might try to sleep herself, only her body felt wound tight as a bow, and she didn't think she'd be able to loosen up enough even to lie back. Finally deciding to rifle through Mrs. Landry's basket more from boredom than hunger, she reached down to lift the lid and see what the lady had packed. Just as her hands gripped an apple, the carriage jerked suddenly and sent her flying headfirst into the viscount's lap.

Her head came up in time to see his eyes snap open seconds before he'd reached down and pulled her up as though she weighed nothing at all.

"I-I'm sorry," she gasped, trying to keep her wits about her. Not easy when she was sprawled atop him, skirts askew, pressed against every hard, solid part of him. "I was just—you were asleep, and I didn't want to wake you, but I was bored, so I thought to check what Mrs. Landry had packed. But the carriage jolted, and I—"

"And you landed on top of me," he finished unhelpfully.

"I'm sorry," she repeated, earning herself a sudden, wicked grin.

"Don't be," he drawled. "Trust me, love, there are far worse ways to wake up."

Elodie's heart stuttered at the casual endearment.

"And if you're bored," he continued, the fire in his eye turning her knees to the consistency of treacle, "there are plenty of ways I can think of to pass the time."

Without warning, he lifted her again, eliciting a squeal from Elodie.

She landed more fully in his lap, her legs sprawled on either side of his.

Her eyes widened at the feel of his hardness against her core, and desire swift and potent exploded inside her. His soft growl indicated that he was experiencing something similar.

"What are you doing?" she asked.

"What sort of escort would I be if I didn't make your journey as entertaining as possible, Elodie?" he whispered, his lips moving tantalizingly closer to her own.

"B-but we can't."

The objection was as weak as her will to really stop him.

But this wasn't what she wanted!

All she wanted was to get to London, hide for a few weeks, and then perhaps find a gentleman who wanted her forever. Though her chances of having the time to do anything other than keep Hope on a leash were, she knew, almost none.

And the viscount didn't want her forever. He'd made that abundantly clear.

The sting of rejection and acute disappointment gave Elodie the strength to pull back from him just a little.

"This isn't at all proper," she said as piously as possible for someone sitting with a man between her legs. "We really must—"

"Let me ask you something," he interrupted. "When was the last time you did something you wanted to do, with no thought to your family name, or your sisters' behavior, or someone else's feelings?"

His question brought her up short, and she frowned at him as she considered her answer.

"Yesterday," she finally said. "When I stowed away in your carriage."

His smile was a thing of beauty. It really wasn't fair. He already had so much; he didn't need to be so utterly handsome, too.

"And I'd wager that as soon as you're with your tearaway family again, you'll fall right back into the role of mother hen, devoting all your time to keeping your sisters in check and doing nothing for yourself?"

She wanted to deny it, but how could she when he was right?

"If this is to be your only break, your only taste of freedom, why not just do what you want without thought to anything else?"

Oh, it was so tempting. *He* was so tempting.

But a lifetime of innate sense and virtue wasn't so easily dismissed.

"Because that's not possible for a lady of quality, Lord Brentford. Everything we do has consequences. One small mistake can lead to irreparable damage."

The irony of her lecturing him on propriety whilst straddling him in a moving carriage wasn't lost on Elodie, and she was suddenly awash with that shame she'd felt after their kiss last night.

It was so easy for him and his ilk.

Rich, powerful men held the world in their hands and could do almost anything without a second thought.

But women—women were held to such exacting standards that even an innocent fall in a courtyard could bring about their destruction.

It was grievously unfair.

*Goodness, I'm beginning to sound like Cheska,* Elodie thought distractedly.

"Only if someone knows about it," he countered swiftly. "And we already know how good we both are at keeping secrets."

The wicked glint she was coming to recognize appeared in the cobalt depths of his eyes, and Elodie felt her flimsy resolve crumble in its wake.

There was no hope for her it seemed.

She would never again lecture Hope on propriety.

Yet underneath the desire was the nagging, hurtful thought— he wanted a secretive interlude but would never want anything more. He'd left her. She'd never be anything more than a covert, temporary problem.

Of course, their relationship could go no further than a few, stolen kisses. No matter how passionate they were.

She had no intention of throwing away the life she'd runaway to start before it even began.

So the question was, how much did she want that fiery, albeit temporary, passion? And was she brave enough to reach out and grasp it?

# Chapter Twenty-One

CHRISTIAN'S ENTIRE BODY felt hard with arousal as he waited impatiently for Elodie's capitulation.

His dreams had been so erotic, so sinful, that to be woken by her in his lap had shaken him to his core.

He'd already been willing to sell his soul to the devil for another taste of her since finding her gazing up at him from the floor, but to have her atop him now, so tantalizingly close that her floral scent surrounded him, was more than he could bear.

It scared the wits out of him. Not just the desire, more potent than any he'd ever experienced. But he just *liked* her so damned much.

She had a sharp wit and a sharper tongue that she kept well hidden beneath her perfect debutante polish.

And her innocence brought out a protectiveness in him that was new and terrifying.

More and more, he was starting to think maybe he'd been too hasty in leaving her behind in Halton.

And that was all the more reason he should be putting distance between them now and not on the verge of begging her to come closer.

But trying to stop wanting her was akin to trying to stop breathing, and the fight was going out of him.

He'd assured her that whatever happened between them on this trip would be secret. And he would take her secrets to the grave.

But a part of him was inclined to think maybe he didn't have to walk away from her when he saw her safely to Town.

Maybe a goodbye wasn't such a certainty anymore.

Distracted as he was by his unexpected thoughts, it took a moment for Christian to notice the new emotion clouding her dark eyes.

He could have sworn there was a flicker of sadness in their depths, and the pang of concern he felt at it almost took his breath away.

Without conscious thought, he reached up and cupped her neck, running his thumb along her cheek, wanting to give her comfort.

"Let go of that control, Elodie," he encouraged quietly. "Don't overthink. Just do what you want. What will make you happy."

He could probably seduce her, he thought with no small amount of conceit, but he'd meant what he said.

Elodie Templeworth had had a lifetime of putting others' needs and wants before her own. So, whatever happened between them now, and he dearly hoped it would be close to what he'd been dreaming about, Christian wanted it to be her decision.

He knew, of course, that tupping was out of the question.

He wasn't trying to completely ruin the girl.

But she was so damned tempting. And he had the strength not to let things get too far.

Didn't he?

The air seemed to freeze around them as Elodie looked at him, her impossibly big eyes searching. For what, he didn't know, but he desperately hoped she'd find it.

She pushed against his chest, and he automatically loosened his hold on her.

Wordlessly, she moved off him and returned once more to the bench she'd been occupying, and Christian had to clench his hands to keep from reaching over and dragging her back.

She'd made her decision, and he had to respect it, even if it meant he'd be walking uncomfortably for hours.

"Shall we?"

Her softly spoke question confused him until he realized that the carriage had come to a stop.

He'd been so caught up in her that he hadn't even noticed they'd arrived at the inn they intended to rest at for a couple of hours.

And judging from the self-satisfied smirk playing around her plump lips, the little vixen knew it, too.

Her power over him was growing. There was no denying it.

Before he could speak, a discreet knock sounded on the door, and Christian reached forward to open it and disembark.

Perhaps some fresh air would clear his suddenly addled mind.

ELODIE TRIED NOT to let her inner turmoil show as she held onto Christian's arm while walking toward the inn.

The rain had stopped finally, though the ground beneath her boots was still sodden and muddy.

She picked her way carefully over the puddles, praying that the mud wouldn't splatter her violet carriage dress too much.

She would have to ask the viscount to have one of her trunks brought to her when they stopped, so she could get some clean garments.

Christian was as attentive and gentlemanly as she could possibly want, and Elodie's heart skittered when he wrapped an impossibly strong arm around her waist and lifted her over a particularly large puddle.

The inn they entered was clean and pleasant. And emptier than Mrs. Landry's had been.

The rain hadn't driven people inside, it seemed, and after a brief conversation with the reed-thin proprietor, Elodie found herself once more ensconced in a perfectly comfortable dining room.

After a quiet maid had seen to them and left them settled alone, Elodie felt it safe to look at the viscount.

She wondered if she'd ever get used to being caught in that ice-blue gaze.

Probably not, she conceded.

And then realized that barring the odd Society event they might both find themselves attending, the chances were that she'd be unlikely to see it very much after the end of their week of travel.

Her stomach grumbled uncomfortably at the thought.

She wasn't likely to be much in the same lauded circles as the Brentford family, she knew.

"What's on your mind?" he asked pleasantly from across the small dining table at which they sat.

"I was thinking of the Season," she replied with as much equilibrium as she could muster. "It's to be my second. Hope's first."

Elodie couldn't prevent a slight shudder at the idea of letting Hope loose on London, and judging by the wry twist of Christian's mouth, he, too, was thinking of the blonde beauty's future in Town.

"I'm sure she won't do too much damage with you watching over her," he drawled casually, but Elodie noticed a tinge of hardness under the polite veneer.

"You think I am too watchful?" she questioned curiously.

"No, I think you shouldn't have to be the one doing the watching," he said with abrupt honesty. "I think you are as entitled to fun as anyone else and that it is not your job to keep your sister in line."

He paused while she swallowed her shock at his words. He seemed quite adamant about it, and she remembered that they'd argued about this very thing only days ago.

"Perhaps an army general would be more suited to the task," he tacked on lightly, and she couldn't help but smile.

"I'm sure I'll manage," she answered.

"But why should you have to?" he demanded, sitting forward suddenly in his seat. "You cannot be much older than your sister?"

"Two years," she answered simply, surprised again at the vehemence in his tone.

"Yet your family would have you act as some sort of spinster sibling, responsible for the care of your sisters."

Elodie's jaw dropped at his hurtful comment.

"You think me a spinster sibling?" she spluttered.

"No, I think you a young, vivacious, and beautiful woman who should only be concerned with enjoying herself."

"How do you know that I don't enjoy myself by taking care of them?" she bit, still smarting from the spinster reference.

"Do you?" he countered.

*No.*

The honest answer whispered inside Elodie's head, but she'd rather stick pins in her eyes than answer him truthfully.

Instead, she heaved a sigh and tried to bring the conversation back to a place at which she was somewhat comfortable and in control of herself.

"I've already had my first Season," she said by way of giving a direct answer. "It is Hope's turn."

"You had your Come Out only last year?" he asked.

Elodie nodded in response.

"I wasn't much interested in it at all, truth be told. But Mama was adamant that I should catch myself a rich husband on the marriage mart."

She fidgeted with the edge of the linen tablecloth.

"I delayed it as long as possible before she dragged me up there," she grinned. "Hope, on the other hand, cannot wait for it. I've never been particularly interested in the pomp and circumstance, the balls and dances and courtships. So it's no matter to me that some may see me as a spinster."

Christian shook his head.

"I didn't call you a spinster," he said.

She opened her mouth to issue a biting retort, but he continued before she had the chance.

"You weren't interested in courtships?" he fired at her, and she began to feel like she was being interrogated by a Bow Street Runner.

"No, not particularly," she answered hesitantly, wondering what he was looking so intense for.

"But you had admirers. Suitors."

It wasn't a question, more a statement of fact.

"How would you know?" she asked, a little uncomfortable under his watchful scrutiny. "Weren't you on the other side of the world then?"

He smiled swiftly.

"I know because I have eyes, Elodie. And I know men, base creatures that we are. There's no way in hell you didn't attract attention. A lot of it."

She was unaccountably flattered that he assumed she had had a vast number of suitors, and he was right in some respect. In the first couple of weeks, her dance card had been filled every evening, invitations came through thick and fast, and afternoon callers had been abundant along with the usual posies of flowers, chocolates, and even on occasion, poetry.

But it had all been in vain as far as Elodie went.

Though Mama had tried her hardest to make her pick a beau, they'd all seemed to be almost exact copies of the same tedious, superficial dandies.

And after days and days of polite but firm rejections, the visitors had petered off, the poetry had mercifully dried up, and they'd stopped having to find vases for the flowers.

She'd enjoyed an occasional afternoon ride through Hyde Park here and trips to Gunther's there. But for the most part, she'd been mercifully left to her own devices.

She realized that while she'd been wool-gathering, he'd been awaiting an answer.

"There were some gentlemen who made an interest known," she answered. "But none of them suited, and that was that."

His expression took on a look of satisfaction. Maybe even relief.

But before she could guess its cause, the door opened, and the servant came in with a tray of luncheon things.

"I'm glad," he said softly, cryptically.

And Elodie spent the entire meal wondering what exactly he was glad about.

# Chapter Twenty-Two

IT HAD BEEN hours since she'd spoken to Lord Brentford.

Since the rain had let up, he'd chosen to ride his stallion Ares for some of the way.

For her own part, Elodie was glad of the reprieve.

Their conversation at lunch had been odd, their conversation in the carriage beforehand, even stranger.

Though she knew that he had no interest in her as a marriage prospect, he seemed to be unduly interested in whether or not she'd been courted. More confusing still was his inordinate interest in her life and the role she played in her family. He wasn't wrong in his observations that she rarely had time to relax and have fun, given that she'd taken on the role of keeper to her irascible sisters.

But she'd never *wanted* to be fun and frivolous and free.

Had she?

She felt the beginnings of a headache as her thoughts circled round and round, all of them somehow involving the handsome viscount. Frankly, she was heartily sick of it. The carriage was bumpy and lonely, her thoughts were confusing and concerning given how wanton they became around the man, and she'd never spent this much time away from her family before.

Granted, the break from Mama was quite refreshing, she thought a little guiltily. And Papa had never spoken to her for longer than absolutely necessary, so his company wasn't exactly a great loss. But her sisters… She looked out the window in time to see the viscount urge his steed forward, perhaps to speak to the driver.

Sophia would be in raptures to see the animal in action.

Even Elodie, who didn't know very much about such things, could appreciate the beauty of the beast.

And the picture Christian painted, tall and strong atop the horse, in complete command.

She heaved a sigh of frustration as her thoughts inevitably went back to him. It was growing ever darker outside, and Elodie hoped they would stop soon. She was tired.

Perhaps this evening, they would be lucky enough to be able to procure two rooms. The distance would be vital to her state of mind.

They couldn't continue as they were.

She was right on the edge of destroying her life, Elodie knew.

Deep down in the most wicked, secret part of her, she knew that every time Christian touched her, she grew closer to her total ruin. Because one day, the conflagration between them would burn so hot that it would burn away the last of her control, the last of her reserve.

He was the only man she'd ever known who could make her think such things, let alone want to act on them.

The carriage drew to a halt before the door suddenly flew open, and there he was, hair windswept from being on horseback, eyes sparkling, charming smile in full effect.

"There is an inn not five miles up the road. If it's acceptable, we'll stop there for the evening?"

Lord, he was so handsome.

Was it any wonder that she'd fallen so easily under his spell?

"Uh, yes," she answered stiffly. "That's perfectly acceptable."

He eyed her speculatively, and she dropped his gaze, unable to hold it for fear that he'd see the depth of her feelings in her own.

But he reached out and gently lifted her chin, forcing her to face him.

"Are you well?" he asked quietly, setting her heart fluttering.

"Of course." She flinched slightly as she heard how she sounded. Exactly as she had during their dance together. "Tired, I suppose."

"It shouldn't take us long to get there," he answered evenly, though she could tell by the slight tightening of his jaw that he didn't believe her.

She nodded, giving him a quick, stilted smile of dismissal.

As the carriage door closed, Elodie felt as though it were closing on something inside of her, too.

Shutting out the possibility of a secret adventure, just for those two.

*I won't tell if you don't.*

Once again, the words floating around her mind.

But it was no use.

Better to suffer the pang of longing now, than the pain of knowing he wanted her—just not enough to make it forever.

SOMETHING WAS WRONG with Elodie.

It came off her in waves. In the stilted answers to his questions. In the way she picked at the venison stew, which had been surprisingly tasty.

He'd procured them two rooms, though it had almost killed him to do so.

But he'd sensed her discomfort in the carriage, and it had been present ever since.

She'd retired to her room as soon as the servants had come to clear the plates, bidding him a mumbled goodnight and fairly flying from the room.

Christian surprised himself by worrying so much about it.

They were playing with fire, he knew. And if they kept it up, one or both of them would get burnt beyond repair.

Yes, she was beautiful and desirable, but so were lots of women.

His mind went to Cressida. Beautiful, willing Cressida.

He hadn't seen her since he'd left for the Americas, but he'd written to tell her of his return home and knew that she was excited to see him from her response.

Cressida played the role of mistress very well. She gave him what he needed sexually whilst making no demands on any other part of his life.

In return, he lavished her in diamonds and furs.

It worked.

It was enough.

Christian swore softly as the words rang hollow and untrue in his head.

He imagined that while he'd been away, Cressida had taken at least one other lover and examined how he felt about that.

Nothing.

He felt nothing.

Then he remembered how he'd felt when he'd thought Elodie was going to marry his cousin. Sick with envy and fiercely angry at the idea of her being hidden away on a farm in the country.

Was it possible that he cared more about the woman he'd met mere days ago than the woman he'd been lying with for almost two years?

Christian jumped to his feet, suddenly restless.

Drinking himself into a stupor, while tempting, probably wasn't very wise.

He should sleep.

But he couldn't stop thinking about Elodie's drawn face, her dark eyes huge and vulnerable.

He needed to know what was wrong; it was as simple as that. He wouldn't rest until he did.

And so, he went to her, refusing to give himself time to question his own sanity.

# Chapter Twenty-Three

CHRISTIAN WASN'T PARTICULARLY worried about anyone seeing him at Elodie's door.

They'd kept up their ruse of being married, but because it was common for members of the peerage to sleep in separate rooms from their spouses, nobody questioned his request for two chambers.

For a brief moment, he allowed himself to imagine if Elodie was truly his viscountess and knew that he'd tear down the walls between them rather than allow her to sleep anywhere but in his arms.

And that thought was the exact reason why he shouldn't be standing here now.

Yet here he stood.

Listening to the sound of movement in the room beyond, he waited, unaccountably nervously for her to open the door.

And then—she was there.

Her eyes widened, and she scrambled to tie the robe that hung loosely over her nightgown.

He watched in fascination as the blush that made a frequent appearance around him stained her cheeks.

"L-Lord Brentford," she stammered. "I thought you were the maid."

"Just me," he quipped casually though desire slammed into him hard and swift at the sight of her unbound hair. "Though I'm more than happy to play at being your maid if you'd like."

His teasing, rather than lightening the tension that emanated from her, seemed to make it worse, and her shoulders stiffened in response.

"Elodie, what's wrong?" he asked, dropping the pretense of joviality.

"Nothing is wrong." She addressed her response to his loosened cravat. "I'm tired, that's all."

Christian felt his ire rising at her obvious lie.

"Something changed in that carriage today," he insisted. "And you haven't been the same since. So please, just tell me."

Suddenly her gaze snapped up to his, and he caught a glimpse of that fire she usually kept banked.

His entire body surged in response.

"Why?"

Thrown by the question, he could only frown down at her.

"What?"

"Why?" she repeated.

"Why, what?"

This was ridiculous, and she seemed to realize that, too, for she huffed out an impatient breath.

"Why do you want me to tell you? Even if something were troubling me, why do you want to know? Why do you care?"

Her question lanced at him, and he didn't know how to answer her.

Why *did* he care?

He could give her some throwaway answer. Smile, make a joke. Bid her goodnight and remind himself that in days he'd be back in London. Back to Cressida and the life he had before he'd ever set foot near the Templeworth family.

But looking into the deep, dark pools of her eyes, he couldn't do it.

All he had for her was honesty.

"I don't know," he answered coarsely. "But somehow, I find that I do."

The words felt wrenched from him, from the very depths of him.

She stood perfectly still, studying him.

Finally, she took a shuddering breath, then shrugged.

"I don't know what you want from me," she confessed, and Christian felt like an utter bastard. Because truth be told, he didn't know what he wanted from her either.

"Neither do I."

ELODIE WANTED TO close the door in his face.

She *should* close the door in his face.

After all, here he was demanding answers but not offering anything in return.

Did he care so little about her, about her reputation?

No, she conceded. He was doing his utmost to protect that. And he didn't have to. He hadn't exactly agreed to having her as a traveling companion, after all.

But her feelings? Her heart? He really didn't care about either of those things.

And yet, despite the sermons and sternly worded lectures she'd given herself all evening, she couldn't stop from wanting him to kiss her again. It felt as though her body craved his. As though she needed him more than she needed to breathe clean air.

Men like the viscount could bed as many women as they liked, not having to worry about consequences, not having to carry the burden of shame for acting on desire.

Should she take the opportunity to enjoy his kisses?

Should she give herself over to temptation, just this once, for this moment out of time?

Her heart squeezed painfully at his brutal honesty.

Some small, idiotic part of her had hoped that he'd tell her he had fallen in love with her. Because fool that she was, she knew that she'd fallen in love with him.

And that's why he was so devastatingly irresistible to her now.

Not because she was a lightskirt or a wanton hussy.

He would never be what she wanted.

Once they got to Town, they would go their separate ways, and Elodie would have to either choose to remain on the shelf, becoming that spinster he'd accused her of being or picking a husband who would never invoke in her the feelings Lord Brentford did.

Her body knew that she'd decided before her mind could catch up.

Without conscious thought, she swayed toward him.

With a dark oath, he reached out and snatched her toward him, his mouth covering hers in a kiss that sealed her fate.

# Chapter Twenty-Four

ELODIE FELT CHRISTIAN'S strong arms wrap around her as she was flung into the maelstrom of desire.

Christian moved one hand down to grab her leg and hitch it around his waist, and instinctively, Elodie moved the other to do the same.

The contact between his hardness and her aching core caused her to moan against his lips, as an answering growl shuddered through him. His tongue plunged inside her mouth, his teeth nipped at her lips, and Elodie didn't know which sensation drove her wilder. They were moving, Christian in complete control, battering her senses with his touch and his taste.

Suddenly Elodie found herself tumbling back, gasping as she hit the mattress of her bed.

"God, you're so beautiful," Christian's voice was agonized as he reared up to stare down at her.

He looked like a ravenous, wild animal, and Elodie's insides clenched as she took in the expression.

"I want to see you," he growled before bending his head to lick the curve of her neck.

His teeth grazed her skin, moving up to bite gently on her earlobe.

Her breath stopped dead in her throat as one hand moved to undo the ties on her nightrail, lifting his mouth from her neck.

All ability to think had fled at her first contact between them, and Elodie voiced no objection as his expert hands pulled the material down, baring her breasts to his gaze.

"So beautiful," he repeated before his lips descended again.

He kissed her hard and fast on the mouth once before he was on the move once more.

His tongue and lips sent her into a frenzy, moving lower and lower still, licking at her collarbone before moving on. When he finally reached her aching breast, the jolt of pleasure was so strong that her lips lifted of their own accord, and he groaned against her flesh as she came into contact with the hard length of him.

She was wiggling beneath him, desperately searching for something she couldn't name.

All she knew was that the pleasure was becoming almost painful, and she knew that only he could give her what she needed.

"Please," she gasped as he laved first one breast, then the other. "Please, Christian. I need... I want..." She didn't know the word. Didn't know how to voice the agonizing need pulsing through her veins. All inhibitions gone, she pressed her lips firmly against him, and he cursed, low and fluidly against her flesh.

Suddenly he reared up and divested himself of his jacket, then waistcoat.

Elodie watched, enthralled as he reached down and pulled the lawn shirt over his head, baring himself to her.

Her mouth dried at the sight of him.

He was beautiful—every inch of him.

Her eyes raked greedily over the broad shoulders, the defined biceps, the rippled muscle of his stomach.

She could have spent hours just drinking in the sight of him, but when her hands moved up to hesitantly rest against his chest before moving lower, lower to the waist of his breeches, his control seemed to snap, and his mouth was on her own again, his tongue plunging inside.

She felt his hand, large and scorching hot, search under the fabric of the nightgown that had ridden up.

His fingers stroked the inside of her thighs, and she almost saw stars.

Her core throbbed with every beat of her heart, and she wasn't sure she'd survive what he was doing to her.

His kiss went on and on, and then suddenly, his hand was right there. Right at the core of her need.

She moaned, and he swallowed the sound as his fingers parted her folds, and his thumb found the secret part of her that had her screaming out, her thighs opening instinctively, her body silently begging for more.

Elodie wrenched her lips from his.

"Christian," she gasped, clawing helplessly at his shoulders, digging her nails into his back, trying to find something steady to hold on to as a storm whipped up inside her.

And just when she thought there couldn't be more, he pushed a finger inside her—moving slowly at first, then more intensely. The coil snapped, and with an uninhibited moan, Elodie's body exploded in a starburst of bliss.

She opened her eyes to find him watching her, the fire in his eyes burning brighter than she'd ever seen it.

He looked tortured but strangely satisfied, and he smiled as he lowered his mouth to take hers in a tender kiss.

When he finally broke away, she heaved a sigh.

"That was…" She shook her head, unable to find the words to describe how she felt.

Besides, his smug expression indicated that he knew exactly the joy he'd given her.

Elodie wondered if she should feel embarrassed, ashamed of how she'd lost control of herself in his arms.

But there was no room for shame.

Only joy.

"You're incredible," he said softly, his hand moving to stroke her face. "I knew there was a fire inside you, Elodie Temple-worth."

She shifted under his admiring gaze, her thigh rubbing against him, eliciting a pained hiss.

"D-did I hurt you?" she asked in concern, sitting up and pulling the edges of her nightrail together, suddenly shy.

His laugh was gruff.

"No, love. You didn't hurt me. You're just driving me mad."

"Oh," she said, for want of anything better to say. "How?"

He laughed again and bent to kiss her.

"By breathing the same air as I," he quipped.

She still didn't know what he meant, but his mouth was upon hers again, and the ability to think was quickly disappearing.

"I have to go," he suddenly said against her lips.

Elodie pulled back to stare at him.

"Go?" she repeated. "But…"

"If I don't go now, I won't be able to go at all," Christian said gently.

Elodie wanted to ask him to stay, but so much had happened…

Perhaps it was best that there be some distance between them.

Christian watched her closely before bending down and placing a tender kiss upon her brow.

"Sleep, love," he said softly, the endearment causing her belly to flip. "I'll see you in the morning."

Elodie didn't speak as she watched him gather his belongings, then slip from the chamber.

Should she feel ruined? Should she regret the liberties he'd taken?

Perhaps so.

But all she could bring herself to feel was pure, unadulterated joy.

# Chapter Twenty-Five

CHRISTIAN STOOD BY the carriage awaiting the arrival of Elodie, his mind in turmoil, his body aching.

He had slept fitfully—his dreams filled with her, her scent clinging to his skin.

Where he'd found the strength to walk away from her, he would never know. But he had and had regretted it ever since.

Perhaps he wasn't quite the soulless bastard he'd imagined, for it would have been so tempting to go further. Sink into her tight heat and lose himself in a way that he knew would be more than anything he'd ever felt before.

He'd never been as aroused as he'd been last night. He'd never come so close to losing every thread of control.

God, but the sounds of her moans were etched in his brain forever.

Yes, he regretted it. And he didn't.

She needed the chance to be happy. To find a husband.

Christian's gut clenched at the idea of her with another man. Her body coming apart in someone else's embrace. Her belly round with another man's children.

The mild envy he'd felt when he'd thought Philip might propose was nothing compared to the jealousy that coursed through him at that thought.

"Damn it all," he whispered though there was nobody around to hear him.

It was the crack of dawn, and no one, bar some servants and stable hands, was stirring.

Elodie was likely still asleep.

Christ, but he was ridiculous.

If he didn't get his body under control soon, he'd embarrass himself in front of the inn staff.

He was going to spend the day on Ares. Spending the day getting some much-needed distance from Elodie and the confusing, terrifying feelings she evoked.

He never had gotten to the bottom of what had bothered her yesterday, being as deliciously side-tracked as he'd been.

But he still wanted to know.

A noise by the door of the inn caught Christian's attention, and he turned his head to see Elodie appear, a vision in violet velvet.

He wanted quite desperately to go to her.

So, he forced himself to stay where he was.

She walked to his side, regal as a queen, and stopped mere inches from him, ensuring that he'd be tormented by that floral scent all day.

He watched her face, saw the heat bloom across her cheeks, noticed how she avoided his gaze.

And he could only imagine what thoughts were rioting around in that head of hers.

The idea of her feeling uncomfortable or in any way ashamed was anathema to him, and so, despite his promises to himself to keep his distance, he reached out to tilt her chin up, forcing her eyes to meet his own.

"Good morning, love," he said with a smile, noting with no small amount of satisfaction that her breath hitched at the action. "How did you sleep?"

Her mouth twisted in a way that he found incredibly endearing.

"I didn't," she answered bluntly. "You?"

"I didn't either," he grinned. "Far too many distracting

thoughts."

Her cheeks grew scarlet under his scrutiny.

And even though he'd decided only moments ago to keep away from her, when he handed her into the carriage, he followed her right in.

CHRISTIAN STAYED IN the carriage for the entire day, meaning that Elodie had no escape from the all-consuming presence of him.

And inevitably, she tumbled further into love with him.

How could she not when he was so charming? So witty?

He told her about his business ventures in the Americas, about his Grand Tour in Europe, and how his visit to Halton came about.

The mention of Philip brought about a cessation to the easy-going manner with which they'd been conversing, at least for Elodie. But it wasn't long before Lord Brentford had her laughing and chattering happily once again.

She regaled him with tales of her sisters' escapades over the years and unknowingly charmed him with her confusion about the male attention she'd received during her Season the year before.

"You really have no idea, do you?" he asked with a smile.

"About what?" she asked.

"How utterly irresistible you truly are, Elodie Templeworth."

How was a lady to keep her heart in her own possession when he said such things? It would take a stronger one than Elodie, in any case.

They stopped at a rather nondescript but clean inn for luncheon, where there was no private dining room available.

Christian insisted that they find somewhere else; Elodie insisted that they stay and dine in the main room.

And so they stayed.

They were just sharing a pot of tea after a pleasant meal when Christian suddenly jumped to his feet.

"That's it. We're leaving."

Elodie stared in shock at the thunderous expression on Christian's face.

"Is something wrong?" she asked.

"Yes, something is damn well wrong," he growled, and her mouth popped open.

He was furious. Though given the fact that he was glaring across the inn, she knew his anger wasn't directed at her.

"Christian, what—"

"Come on," he reached down and grasped her arm, pulling her gently from her seat. Reaching into his pocket, he dropped a bag of coins on the table before moving her swiftly through the inn and out into the courtyard.

Once outside, Elodie pulled her arm from his grip, frowning up at him in consternation.

"What on earth are you about?" she snapped, her body still reeling from even that simplest of contact from him.

"We needed to get out of there," he answered as though he hadn't just acted like a madman.

"But why?"

"Because if one more man had drooled over you like a dog in heat in there, I would have torn his eyes from his head. That's why."

Once more, Elodie could only stare at him.

Not only because she'd rarely heard such coarse language, especially directed to her, but because she'd never seen him so angry. Not even when he'd discovered her in his carriage.

"I didn't notice any undue staring," she said soothingly, trying to placate him while wondering at the source of such fury.

"Well, I damn well did," he answered, evidently not in the mood to be placated. "And it's no surprise you didn't notice in any case," he ranted, his expression almost accusatory. "How can you be so oblivious to your own appeal, Elodie? How can you not know that you could bring a man to his knees with just a look?"

She didn't know what to say.

She was rendered completely speechless, both by his incredible words and the desperation they awoke in her.

Why could he not truly mean what he said? At least for himself. Why did he call her irresistible, yet he could not want her for himself?

Watching him as she was, she saw the light of anger bleed from his eyes to be replaced by something far more wicked, far more dangerous.

"Like that," he groaned as though he were in pain. "That look right there."

"I don't…I didn't…"

She didn't know what to say, so she drew to a stop.

And suddenly, he moved. His hands came up to capture her face.

"No, you don't do it on purpose," he said gruffly. "You're too genuinely good for that. But you do it all the same, Elodie. I'm a slave to those eyes."

And before she could respond, before she could remind him that they were in a very public courtyard and therefore liable to be seen, he pulled her toward him and claimed her mouth in a kiss that shattered her.

# Chapter Twenty-Six

CHRISTIAN GAVE ARES his head, thundering ahead of his carriage and the woman inside it.

Perhaps kissing her so publicly at the inn earlier that day hadn't been his wisest decision.

But the longer he spent with her, the more utterly irresistible she became to him.

While they'd been dining, he'd tried to concentrate only on her. He really had.

But every time he so much as glanced away, it seemed there was a new set of lecherous eyes staring in her direction. And so Christian, who'd never been jealous in his life, had become so murderous that he'd had to drag her out and away from the men in that inn.

Cressida, he knew, had had countless lovers before him and would have more when he was gone.

Why didn't that bother him at all?

Cursing himself, Christian eased the stallion to a canter, then a trot.

It wouldn't do to bring his horse up lame just because he was trying to stay ahead of Elodie.

He turned back to the coach, telling the driver that he would ride ahead and procure lodgings.

And as he rode into the stable, he found himself wondering whether he wanted them to have two rooms available, or whether he wanted more than anything for Elodie to have to spend the night with him again.

Elodie sighed as she lay back in the hot bath.

Dinner had been excruciating.

After their explosive kiss in the stable, Christian had handed her into the carriage, and she hadn't seen him again until they'd stopped here for the night.

Thankfully, he'd been able to procure a private dining room, but he'd been silent and brooding, his eyes more on the brandy he'd been drinking than on her.

When she'd left to bathe and retire, he'd bid her a swift goodnight.

She'd felt his eyes on her as she'd walked away.

And then she'd sat there as the maids filled her bath, pretending not to hear their giggles about the viscount, about his handsomeness and his charm, and how they hoped to catch a glimpse when they went to fill the bath he'd requested for himself.

She'd been torn between wanting to blister their ears and wanting to tiptoe in there to get a look for herself.

She was a hopeless case.

In two days, they'd be in London.

Was the rest of their time together to be spent with him ignoring her existence?

Granted, this escapade had never been about spending time with Christian. He'd been a means to an end, an escape route when she'd desperately needed one.

But she *had* spent time with him, and now she couldn't bear the idea of not seeing him again.

Perhaps she'd been too forward. Regardless of her behavior having been good or bad, she worked herself up.

Climbing out of the tub, she wrapped her robe around her body and tied it securely, then grabbed a candle from the dresser and, without giving herself a chance to think through her actions, she flung open the door and marched to Christian's room, hammering on his door before she lost her nerve.

She waited, her bare foot tapping impatiently on the cold flagstones as she listened out for sounds in the room.

There was a thud, some shuffling, and then suddenly the door was flung open, and there he stood.

His chest was bare, and his breeches unbuttoned, and Elodie realized he'd most likely been completely naked when she'd first knocked upon his door.

Her throat went dry, the anger that had driven her here began to be replaced by desire, potent and fierce.

"Elodie? What is it? What's wrong?"

She simply stared at him.

"Elodie?"

He reached out and grasped her shoulders, shaking her a little.

"Are you hurt? Did someone upset you? Tell me!"

The touch of his hands on her shoulders brought her out of her daze, and she scowled up at him.

"Yes, someone upset me," she snapped. "You."

"Me?" He was incredulous, and for some reason, that made Elodie angrier.

"Yes, you," she answered, poking him in the chest.

Well, that had been a mistake. Now her finger tingled as though she'd been burned.

"You are a hypocrite."

He went from shocked to furious in seconds.

"How?" he demanded.

A noise sounded at the end of the corridor, reminding Elodie that they were arguing in a very public hallway.

Christian obviously noticed, too, for with a muffled curse, he pulled her into his room, then kicked the door shut behind her.

"Right, how am I a hypocrite?" he repeated, arms folded and face scowling.

He looked darkly, dangerously handsome, and Elodie was finding it harder to concentrate, but she couldn't allow him to distract her.

"You've ignored me all afternoon," she said, hearing the hurt lacing her voice but unable to control it. "And I can only assume it's because you have deemed my behavior unladylike and…and immoral. But I feel I should tell you that if that is the case, then yes, you are a hypocrite. For you have kissed me, too. You have…have…well, you know," she stumbled, feeling the heat of embarrassment scald her cheeks as she thought back on last night. "And I should keep in mind if I were you that I have never even kissed a gentleman before you. However, you, I'm quite certain, have not lived like a monk."

He'd dropped his hands now, but she noticed they were balled into fists at his sides.

"So—so if that *is* the cause of your distance then…then that is grievously unfair."

She huffed out a breath as she came to an end of her rant, watching him as he watched her.

The silence stretched on enough that Elodie started to feel a bit awkward, and she thought it best if she just scurried off.

She only had one more night in his company after tonight. She could survive one night and two days of his rudeness.

The sting of rejection, the heartache of their upcoming distance—that would be harder to survive.

He still hadn't moved, so heaving a sigh, Elodie turned to leave.

She hadn't even taken a full step when suddenly his arm was upon her, spinning her to face him.

"You think I've been distanced because I've been *judging* you?" he asked, his tone disbelieving, his face furious.

"I know you have," she threw at him.

"Nothing could be further from the truth, Elodie," he ground out. "I've been keeping my distance because I can't keep my damned hands off you."

"Nobody asked you to do that."

"And you have no idea what you're getting yourself into," he barked.

"Don't shout at me."

"I'm not shouting," he yelled.

They both drew to a stop, glaring at each other.

"You need to leave."

Elodie would have been hurt at the demand if his face didn't look so pained saying it.

"You want me to go?" she asked softly.

His laugh held no humor.

"No, I don't want you to go," he said. "Which is exactly why you should."

*Listen to him, Elodie,* she told herself. *He's right. This path you're walking is too dangerous. Turn around and walk away.*

She couldn't do it, though.

She couldn't force herself to turn and walk away from him.

"Elodie."

Her name sounded as though torn from his lips.

Still, she did not move.

And then he was there, falling on her as though he'd been starved of the taste of her.

The candlestick clattered to the ground, unnoticed by either of them.

He lifted her from her feet, his lips already stealing any thoughts outside of him and this moment she might have.

# Chapter Twenty-Seven

S HE WAS GOING to be the death of him, Christian knew. But he could think of no better way to go.

Laying her on the bed, he told himself he'd be able to resist making her his in every way.

He could do it; he was sure.

And then he looked down at her and knew it would take great strength. Strength he didn't even know if he possessed.

Now was the time to tell her to go. To say it and mean it.

But then she smiled up at him, her lips curling in unconscious sensuality.

And the control that he'd been ever in danger of losing snapped.

Nothing could drag him from her now. Not his distaste for commitment, not the knowledge of her innocence and purity. Nothing.

He ravished her mouth, his hands making light work of the ties of her robe.

The robe fell open, and Christian couldn't contain his oath as he realized she wore nothing beneath it.

He'd been so shocked, so angered by her claim that he somehow found her wanting that he hadn't even noticed.

Sitting back, he gazed down at her with reverence.

How could she think he judged her? Thought her anything less than perfect? It was madness.

Her tiny hands reached up to wrap around his neck and pull his head toward her, and he realized, with no small amount of satisfaction, that she was as ravenous for him as he was for her. He kissed her with abandon, wishing to devour her—to possess her.

There was an edge to her movements this evening, a new depth to her passion, and he relished every second of it.

"Christian?"

He lifted his head, curious about the hesitancy in her tone.

If she asked him to stop, he would, but it would kill him.

"Yes, love?" He gritted his teeth against the feel of her hips pressing against him.

"Last night… What you d-did?"

Damn it, he felt like he was going to spill his seed just watching her nibble nervously at her bottom lip.

"Don't worry," he grinned. "There's plenty more where that came from."

Her eyes widened in the most adorable way, and his heart twisted, momentarily distracting him from the physical ache. Something he wouldn't have said was even possible.

He felt a rush of tenderness, foreign and intense.

Surely it wasn't love. It couldn't be!

"I wasn't going to ask that," she sniffed, and he marveled at how she could sound so innocent when she was writhing beneath him, her breasts crushed against his chest, her legs opened to accommodate his length.

"I just wondered…that feeling… Can it happen for you, too?"

Yes, she would most definitely be the death of him.

Clearing his throat, he tried to focus his mind enough to form coherent sentences. Almost an impossibility given the circumstances.

"Something similar, yes," he answered as evenly as he could manage. "It's not quite the same, but it is just as wonderful."

"And I can do that? For you?"

That did it.

That was the thing that pushed him over the edge.

With a groan of defeat, Christian once again captured Elodie's mouth.

To hell with his former ideas about commitment, love, marriage, and the rest of it.

Every other thing in his life paled in that moment, their importance burned away by the fire of his desire for this woman.

Let the chips fall where they may.

He couldn't stop it now, this raging thing between them.

And right now, he didn't want to.

"You can, love. Later," he said against her mouth. "Right now, I need to taste you."

And he set about doing just that.

ANY EMBARRASSMENT OR horror Elodie might have been feeling disappeared at the first touch of Christian's tongue.

The ache that he'd awoken in her from his first kiss exploded in a riot of feeling, wrenching a cry from her lips as her hips shot off the bed.

Christian's hands clamped down on them, anchoring her to the bed while he continued his ministrations.

She was mindless. Squirming.

And still it went on.

Elodie wasn't sure how much more she could take, how much longer she could survive, and then she felt a finger slip inside her, and she shattered into a thousand pieces.

He had brought her to heaven, and she wanted the same for him. She wanted to share it with him.

Having grown up in the countryside, Elodie wasn't entirely clueless as to how certain things could happen.

"Christian," she whispered and, gathering up what little courage she had, she reached down and palmed him through his breeches.

His response was instantaneous, his growl guttural as he thrust into her hand.

"Show me. I want—I want us both to feel it. I want to give you what you've given me."

He leaned on one elbow, using the other to push a tendril of hair from her brow.

"You don't have to, love. It's enough for me to—"

"I want to," she burst out, though a part of her was terrified.

There would be no coming back from this. Once she traveled down this path, her life would be set in stone.

No respectable marriage. Likely no loving husband. Maybe even no children.

And yet, she knew she would never feel for anyone the way she felt for this man.

Acting on pure instinct, she wrapped her legs around his waist, pushing against him, delighting in the oath he muffled against the skin of her neck.

"Elodie," he begged. "Stop."

"Don't you want to?" she asked, suddenly worried that she'd done something wrong or that she was less desirable to him than she'd thought.

"Oh sweetheart, you have no idea how much I want to," he said. "But I won't ruin you. I won't take your choices away. There are other ways we can enjoy each other."

She stared up at him.

How did he not know?

He'd already ruined her. Perhaps not physically, but her heart had been very much ruined for any other man.

And that same heart twisted painfully now as she realized that, even now, he clearly didn't want her forever.

But she'd always known that hadn't she?

She'd always known that their time was running out.

So setting aside her heartache for later, when she was alone in London and could examine it and suffer it in her own time, she smiled.

"Other ways?" she asked as lightly as she could. "What might they be."

His answering grin was a thing of sheer, masculine wickedness, and Elodie felt her breath catch at the beauty of it.

"Let me show you," he whispered before taking her mouth in a toe-curling kiss once more.

# Chapter Twenty-Eight

Tonight would be their last together.

Christian was painfully aware of that fact as he sat in his carriage watching Elodie sleep.

She was probably worn out from the evening before, he thought smugly.

Nobody would think looking at her now, her face the picture of feminine innocence, that she was wild and passionate underneath.

He was growing hard just thinking of last night. She was exquisite in every sense of the word. And a hell of a quick study.

He couldn't contain his grin as he thought of the hours they'd spent learning each other's bodies.

Yet no matter how much he'd enjoyed their night together, and he had—more than any he'd ever spent with a woman before—he couldn't stop himself from craving that last step. Making her his, fully and completely. Taking her innocence and keeping it for his own.

A thought had been nagging at him all morning whilst they'd been traveling; if he'd taken responsibility for their unfortunate incident back in Halton, they could be betrothed now for real, instead of pretending. She could be his. And then maybe this unexpected possessiveness wouldn't plague him every second of the day.

Is that what he wanted, though?

He cared for her; there could be no denying it. He felt ridiculously overprotective of her. And he desired her more than any woman he'd ever known.

She made him laugh, she drove him crazy, and he was starting to feel like her happiness was vital to his own.

Wasn't that reason enough to marry?

Could it even be love?

He didn't know. But he'd have to find an answer to his own questions soon.

For their arrival in London was fast approaching.

She had said that she would be quite alone for however long it took her family to arrive in Town.

And then, he knew, she'd have her hands full with those sisters of hers.

A flicker of irritation stirred in him.

He didn't want her spending the entire Season playing governess to the little tearaways.

He wanted her to laugh and dance, to have fun and be frivolous.

And court?

His gut twisted.

No, he didn't want that. Base creature that he was, he didn't want another man anywhere near her.

Sighing, he turned to look out the window at the darkening sky.

They should arrive at their last stop before Town within the hour.

Should he wake her now or leave her to rest?

She stirred in her sleep, her tongue darting out to wet her bottom lip before she settled down once more.

Let her sleep, he decided.

With any luck, she'd be far too busy this evening to get much rest.

ELODIE STIRRED AT the feather-light touch against her skin.

She didn't know if it was a dream, but her stomach flipped in anticipation.

Lips. Those were definitely real lips.

She smiled, not yet opening her eyes, just enjoying the feeling of soft, tender kisses upon her cheek, her neck, her ear.

"Wake up, love. We're here."

*Christian.*

Her eyes fluttered open.

"Come," he said. "Let's get you fed. Then you can sleep."

Hiding a yawn behind her hand, Elodie reluctantly sat up.

She was so tired she could barely keep her eyes open.

Last night, she'd spent hours in Christian's room until he'd carried her back to her own before the servants awakened for morning chores.

They hadn't set out particularly early this morning, but she still couldn't wait for a full night's sleep in a bed.

Her stomach clenched when she realized that after tonight, she would have nothing *but* nights alone in her bed.

But she'd made a pact with herself that her heartache would remain locked away until they said goodbye, and she intended to stick to it.

Losing Christian from her life would be the worst thing imaginable, so adding another layer to that pain couldn't make her feel any sadder.

"If you keep looking at me like that, we won't make it out of this carriage," he warned, his voice deliciously husky.

Nothing could have sounded better to Elodie, and that must have shown on her face, for within seconds, he'd plucked her from her seat into his lap and pressed his lips urgently against her own.

Elodie clung to his shoulders as he ran his tongue along the seam of her lips, forcing them open for the invasion of his tongue.

How would she go without this for the rest of her life? How would she know happiness if it wasn't by his side?

Her thoughts were starting to grow fuzzy under Christian's clever ministrations.

"God, how easily you make me lose control," he mumbled against her neck. "You are a temptress, Elodie Templeworth."

He moved his lips from her neck before reaching up to cup her face in both hands.

He stared so intently into her eyes that Elodie felt as though he were looking into her very soul.

"Elodie," his voice was a whisper, but there was a wealth of feeling in it, and her heart started thundering. "I wanted to tell you...I—"

Whatever he'd been about to say was brutally interrupted when the carriage door was suddenly flung open, and Hope, Francesca, and Sophia fell over each other, landing in an undignified heap at their feet.

Elodie screeched, scrambling off Christian's lap and tumbling over her sisters.

"Elodie, hide."

"How can she hide, you dolt? We're in a carriage," Sophia said.

"Apologies, your lordship. I didn't mean to grab your—"

"Hope! Now is not the time. Elle, climb out the window."

"Were you in his lap?"

"You're standing on my skirt. Ouch!" Francesca rubbed her hand down her skirt and frowned.

"She's not going to fit out the window," Hope said.

"Well, it's better than what's facing her out there. Should we all just make a run for it?" Sophia asked.

"Why on earth are you in here and not on that gorgeous mount, Lord Brentford?"

"Sophia, you're *on my skirt.*"

Elodie couldn't make head nor tail of what her sisters were

saying in the cacophony of sounds.

By the time she righted herself and extricated herself from her sisters—who were all screeching, squealing, and screaming over each other—they had gathered a stone-faced audience outside the carriage.

Elodie looked into the grim faces of her mother, father, and here her stomach sank—Philip Harrison.

# Chapter Twenty-Nine

S HE DIDN'T KNOW what to do.

For the first time in her life, Elodie Templeworth—the fixer, the soother, the one who always knew what to say and what to do to smooth over an awkward situation—was completely stuck.

She could only stare.

"We kept them at bay as long as possible," Cheska whispered in her ear. "But Mama was a woman possessed wanting to catch you before you got to London."

"And nobody invited the pig farmer," Hope added with a scowl.

"I'm not entirely sure that Papa noticed you were gone, to be honest," Sophia's voice was far too bright and chatty given the situation, but then she was only twelve years old and had probably not grasped the seriousness of it. "I think he's only here because Mama threatened to steal his carriage."

Still, Elodie couldn't move, couldn't speak.

Helpless and scared, she looked to Christian.

Their time was up, she realized with a pang.

After all, she already knew that he had no qualms in walking away, even at the risk of her reputation being ruined forever.

And he owed her nothing; he'd made no promises.

She'd allowed Lord Brentford to compromise her.

No. Worse. She'd practically *begged* him to compromise her, and it had been his good sense, his moral strength, that had kept her from being completely ruined.

*Or was it his sense of self-preservation?* An ugly voice awoke in her head and would not be silenced.

He hadn't taken her innocence. Once again, he was free to walk away. She was lost in her thoughts, shocked at being caught with him by her parents…

"If you'll excuse me, ladies?"

As casually as if this were a polite meeting in a London ballroom, Christian smiled at them then removed himself from the carriage.

The Templeworth girls fell silent as he magnanimously held out a hand to each of them, helping them all alight from the coach.

It was a quiet and confused procession of girls, and Elodie's parents and Mr. Harrison watched them, speaking not a word.

Finally, it was Elodie's turn.

Wordlessly, Christian reached out a hand, and she placed her own in it, eyes firmly on the ground, mind whirling with riotous emotions.

She felt his hand squeeze her own, and her gaze met his.

"Courage, love," he said quietly.

*Courage.*

The strength to deal with the fallout from all of this when he walked away?

She wanted to be angry with him, but her sadness left no room for any other emotion.

So, lifting her chin, she turned to face her parents.

"Mama, Papa," she said, her voice trembling but clear. "I can explain."

CHRISTIAN'S HEART BURST with pride as he watched Elodie's chin tilt upward.

He knew that she must be quaking in her kid boots, but outwardly she looked as calm and lovely as ever.

And while part of him was rather curious to hear just what she would come up with, another part knew that there was only one way to fix this.

"There is no explaining this, Elodie. How could you? You have destroyed this family. Destroyed our good name and destroyed any chance your sisters have of making respectable matches," her mother said.

He waited for Elodie to defend herself, to remind her selfish mother that she'd lived her entire life worrying about her sisters. More than their parents had, by all accounts.

But she said nothing, just stood there in silence, taking the verbal lashing.

And his temper ignited.

"Mama, I hardly think we need Elodie's help to ruin our chances of a good marriage," one of the blondes piped up, and Christian was glad that *someone* in this insane family seemed to care about Elodie.

"Yes, I'll ruin my own chances, thank you very much," the other sister scowled.

"And I have absolutely no intention of marrying, so don't worry on my account," the little one who looked most like Elodie stated firmly.

Christian felt a wave of affection for the Templeworth girls.

Clearly, the mother's awfulness hadn't rubbed off on her daughters.

"Be quiet, all of you," the woman snapped at her younger daughters. "Elodie, all of our hopes rested on you. How could you be so unfeeling about your sisters? How could you do this to me?"

Right.

That was enough.

"Madam, I suggest you calm yourself," Christian spoke smoothly, keeping as tight a grip on his fury as he could. "I would remind you that it's not Elodie's job to parent your other daughters, it's yours. The responsibility for their behavior rests squarely on your shoulders and yours alone."

The silence was deafening.

Christian could feel every set of eyes on him.

He should perhaps have included the girls' father in his statement, but a quick glance at the man showed he cared not a whit about another man lecturing his wife. Or indeed, about a man being locked away in a carriage with his unmarried daughter.

What the hell sort of father was he?

"Christian—"

Philip stepped forward now, reminding Christian of his presence.

"Why are you even here?" Christian snapped before his cousin could speak.

He was furious that Philip had been included in this.

Were her parents still trying to force a match there? Was Philip so enamored of Elodie that he would overlook all of this just to have her as a wife?

Philip would get to Elodie over his dead body.

"I... I..."

"He's been hanging about like a bad smell ever since Elodie escaped," Francesca Templeworth said, her tone disgusted, and Christian's lips twitched despite the seriousness of their current situation.

Good God, but the Templeworth chits were a handful.

He was shocked that Elodie had been able to keep them in check at all.

"Francesca," the mother hissed, but the young woman seemed marvelously unperturbed.

"I-I'm to be married to her. Mr. Templeworth and I—we... We have an arrangement."

Christian scowled down at his cousin as Philip wiped his sweating brow.

He heard Elodie's gasp behind him at Philip's words but couldn't move as he tried to tamp down his own rage.

What sort of man was Philip in any case, that he'd have her now after all this?

*The same sort as you,* an irritating voice spoke up in his head. *Because you'd do it, too.*

Christian finally allowed himself to drag his eyes from Philip and look at Elodie.

She was deathly pale, her eyes—always his greatest weakness—huge and dark and pained.

And he couldn't let her go.

Regardless of whether or not he understood his own feelings right now, regardless of his disinterest in marriage and fatherhood and continuing his legacy—no part of him felt able to hand this woman over to people who didn't appreciate her enough or care for her enough. People who had no idea about the fiery siren that lay under the veneer of the coolly beautiful angel, and who would never encourage that side of her to come out.

"Then I'm sorry to tell you that your arrangement will have to be rearranged, cousin," Christian spoke to Philip, but he kept his eyes on Elodie. He was taking a risk. A big one. "Because I intend to marry her myself."

# Chapter Thirty

THERE WAS A moment of complete silence before the courtyard burst into chaos. Throughout it all, Christian watched Elodie.

Trying to decipher her feelings was an impossibility. She was a statue, unmoving even when her sisters threw their arms around her.

Was she angry? Did she hate him now?

Surely she could see that there was no other way.

A panic that he'd never felt before in his life rushed through Christian.

Would she run away again? There was no doubt that she'd manage it with her army of sisters behind her.

Was he so bad that she'd run from him? And if she did, would he give chase?

She looked up at him then, and the answer hit him straight through the heart.

Yes, he would. He'd follow her to the ends of the earth.

"Now just a minute." All chatter stopped as Elodie's useless father finally spoke up. "Mr. Harrison and I have had contracts drawn up. You cannot just—"

"Oh, do be quiet, Arthur," Mrs. Templeworth snapped. "A viscountess! Oh, my dear girl, I knew you could do it."

Mr. Templeworth frowned at his wife before shrugging and falling quiet again as his fiercely annoying wife barrelled over and threw her arms around Elodie as though she hadn't just been berating her for them all to hear.

"Mrs. Templeworth, I thought—"

"Not now, Mr. Harrison, please. We have plans to make."

And having well and truly dismissed Philip, she took hold of Elodie and dragged her toward the inn, shouting behind her for her husband to procure a dining room.

Christian could only watch as Elodie was pulled, tight-lipped, toward the building, her gaggle of sisters trailing behind her.

Christian watched Mr. Templeworth run to do his wife's bidding. Watched as Elodie was swallowed in a sea of skirts and shrieks.

He wanted to go to her, to see if she was well. But he needed to get her alone, and that wasn't going to happen any time soon.

Taking a deep breath and unconsciously rubbing at the pain in his heart, he turned to face his cousin.

"Something on your mind, Philip?"

"How did this happen?" Philip exploded, spittle flying from his mouth. "You said you had no interest in her. You said you were leaving. That *I* should offer for the lady."

"And now you don't have to," he answered through gritted teeth.

"You said you didn't want her!" Philip shouted, making Christian feel like a bastard. He had said that. Tried to pass her off on his cousin like an irritation he'd needed to get rid of.

"Well, things change."

"Not that much, they don't," Philip responded with more gumption than Christian would have thought he possessed. "Are you going to tell me you care for her?"

"I'm not going to tell you anything," Christian snapped. He didn't like the reminder of what he'd said about Elodie.

He'd had no idea then what she would come to mean to him in such a short amount of time.

"Well, are you going to tell her then? About your mistresses?"

Christian growled, losing his grip on his temper.

He didn't want to be out here arguing with his cousin.

He wanted to be inside, making sure that Elodie was all right.

And truth be told, he was probably less angry with Philip than he was with himself.

He'd sealed his fate as well as Elodie's, without even speaking to her.

And the thought of having to tell her about Cressida…

He wouldn't continue to see his mistress, of course, he wouldn't. And Philip was right—he should tell her that.

He should tell her a lot of things.

And he was going to. Right now.

"Are you going to join us for luncheon?" he asked, his tone conciliatory.

There was no need for him to be at odds with his cousin, and truth be told, he felt bad for the man.

He must care about Elodie a great deal if he was willing to come all the way here to salvage something between them.

Maybe if Christian cared about her less or could be the bigger man, he'd step aside. But he couldn't. He wouldn't.

Maybe that made him a selfish blackguard, but it wouldn't change his decision.

"You won't make her happy."

Christian stifled a sigh.

They obviously weren't done here.

He reminded himself that Philip was hurting and tried to keep his anger in check.

"And how do you know that?" Christian asked, smugly aware that he'd made her happy in ways the other man could only dream of.

"Because you don't know her. She is quiet, genteel, reserved. She won't be happy with Town life. She won't be happy with anything more than a simple, country life."

Christian laughed.

"No, *you* don't know her, cousin," he parried. "You have never bothered getting to know the real Elodie because you were never interested in the real Elodie. Just the paragon she had no choice but to present herself as."

He could tell from his cousin's expression that the man didn't understand a thing he was saying.

All the more reason that Elodie shouldn't be tied to one such as Philip for life.

"You don't deserve her," Philip snapped.

"Undoubtedly," was Christian's smooth reply. "But neither do you."

He was just turning to leave when Philip's bitter response stopped him in his tracks.

"If I'd known you'd eventually do right by her, I never would have spread the rumor about you two."

It took a moment for Christian to understand the meaning of Philip's words, but when he did, an icy fury swept through his veins.

"You?" he breathed. "But, why? I was leaving. I wouldn't have been in your way."

"I knew she would never have me. Choose me. And I knew you would never want her for yourself. So I thought—"

"You thought if you ruined her life, she'd have no choice but to accept you," Christian spat. "You caused her all that pain, all that shame, just so you could selfishly have her for yourself."

"It's not too late," Philip said rather desperately. "You can forget all this. Give her back."

"Give her back?" Christian repeated furiously. "As though she is nothing more than a piece of property to be passed around? Get the hell out of here, Philip. I don't want you anywhere near her."

"If she'd just bloody well done what she was told—" Philip started but didn't get a chance to finish.

Christian's fist shot out, landing with a satisfactory crack on his cousin's face.

Shaking out his hand, he glared at the man sprawled at his feet.

"If you ever come anywhere near my future wife again, I'll

beat you with my bare hands."

But as blackly furious as he was with his idiotic cousin, he had to wonder if he should be thanking the man instead.

Had Philip's plan worked, Christian wouldn't be on the verge of having Elodie for his wife. But he was.

And he couldn't help but feel grateful for that.

SHE WAS ENGAGED to Christian.

Or was she?

Elodie felt numb.

She allowed herself to be dragged into the inn, away from Christian, by her mother, who was now acting as though Elodie was a queen when only minutes ago she'd felt like dirt beneath her shoe.

And poor Philip. He'd been dragged here, most likely by her mother, who would have figured a gentleman farmer was better than no husband at all for her fallen daughter.

Would he really have married her after all this? Elodie felt a pang of guilt. She had had no idea that Philip held her in such high regard.

Higher than his cousin, clearly. His cousin to whom now she was betrothed.

A part of Elodie, namely her foolish heart, tried its hardest to be elated. Being Christian's wife was beyond any joy she could have ever hoped for.

However, her brain was starting to work again now that the shock was easing, and she knew the truth.

Christian had done the right thing. The gentlemanly thing.

They'd been caught, backed into a corner, and he'd taken the only path that could have salvaged Elodie's life.

And now, because of that, he'd be stuck in a marriage he didn't want, with a woman he didn't love.

Yes, he desired her. He'd made that clear with his body and his words. But desire wasn't love. And moral obligation wasn't love. It wasn't even affection.

Elodie's stomach turned as her mother and sisters babbled and chattered.

Papa had made light work of taking a dining room and had preceded them into it. There was no sign of Christian and Mr. Harrison.

"Elle."

Elodie turned her head automatically at the sound of her name being whispered beside her.

She looked into Hope's concerned eyes.

"Are you well? Is this… Is this what you want?"

Was it what she wanted?

Yes, it was. More than anything. But not like this.

"I didn't want him caught in the parson's trap, no," she answered past the lump in her throat.

Hope watched her closely as her eyes filled with tears.

"You love him."

It was a statement, not a question. It must be obvious to everyone around them.

"I do," she sniffed miserably. "Far too much to feel happy that I've trapped him."

"What are you crying for, you foolish gel?"

Her mother's voice, loud and abrasive, interrupted Elodie's and Hope's conversation.

"You've brought a viscount to heel! Nothing could have been better for us."

At that moment, the door to the dining room opened, and Christian marched in, his face set in a furious mask, his eyes glinting.

And Elodie wanted to cry all over again.

Perhaps nothing would be better for the Templeworths.

But clearly, Christian wasn't happy about it.

She'd ruined his life.

And now, even her heart was miserable.

Because how could she be happy to the detriment of the man she loved?

At that moment, Christian's eyes turned toward her, and Elodie felt a lone tear slip down her cheek.

She watched as he grimaced, his jaw clenched, his eyes dulling with unconcealed pain.

Elodie couldn't stand to look at him for much longer, so she turned away.

# Chapter Thirty-One

CHRISTIAN SCOWLED AS he stood at the edge of the crowded ballroom, wanting nothing more than to make an escape.

The Season had yet to begin, but one wouldn't know that from the packed ballroom in Lord and Lady Dowering's townhouse.

Usually, he'd rather stick pins in his eyes than attend this sort of thing, but since Elodie's blasted mother had gotten her claws into his fiancée, he had to abide by Society rules just to see her.

His fiancée.

It still didn't feel quite real. Not least because it had only happened a week ago, and ever since then, she'd been under the watchful eye of her mother, who had suddenly decided to play the chaperone.

He needed to get her alone. He needed to speak to her and make sure that she was well.

All week he'd been haunted by that lone tear trailing down her cheek. Haunted by how desolate she'd looked sitting across the room from him.

He'd thought, hoped really, that there was affection between them. But her face that day—it destroyed him. And then she'd been swept away by her family, and he'd only seen her when he'd called on her, where her mother fawned over him so much that he couldn't get a word in edgewise, or when he'd taken her riding in Hyde Park where he'd been stopped by so many acquaintances that he couldn't string a sentence together without interruption.

At least tonight, he could dance with her, and dancing meant he could actually hold a conversation with her.

He just needed to know that she was well.

"One would have thought that a recently affianced man would look a little cheerier."

Christian turned his head and found his old friend Jonathan Spencer grinning at him.

Jonathan and Christian had been at Oxford together and, though Jonathan's life had been spent traveling to God knew where, and Christian had been building his business interests in India and the Americas, they had always caught up as and when they could.

"Being engaged is not the problem," Cristian said by way of greeting. "Being unable to get anywhere near my fiancée is."

"Ah, yes. I can imagine."

Christian watched Jonathan's eyes seek out his own wife. He wasn't sure about the details, but he knew Jon and his French wife, Gabrielle, had been separated for a time before they found their way back to each other.

And looking at how smugly satisfied Jonathan seemed as he watched his dark-haired wife weave her way toward him, the time apart hadn't dimmed his friend's love for the lady.

"It's not easy, is it? Looking but not being able to touch?"

Christian's mind immediately went to his week alone with Elodie and all the touching he'd done.

And something of what he was feeling must have shown in his face, for Jonathan snorted and shook his head.

"I wonder if you'll last until the banns are read," he quipped, shaking his head.

Christian was about to answer when a movement at the entrance caught his eye, and there she was.

He'd made sure that Lady Dowering extended an invitation to the Templeworths. Since they weren't peers, he wasn't sure if they were in the Dowering's elite circle.

He needn't have worried, though.

Word had gotten round Town from almost the second he'd arrived that he was engaged, meaning that everyone wanted to know who the lady was.

Elodie had been well and truly thrust into the center of Society's attention, something he knew she wouldn't particularly enjoy.

Her mother, however, was in raptures about it, and her sister Hope already seemed to be making it her mission in life to have men trail her through every event in London.

She was beautiful, of that there was no doubt. And her flirtatious nature ensured that the men of London came to worship her in droves.

Christian didn't understand it, though. How could anyone even notice Hope when Elodie was around?

But then, he reasoned, everyone knew she was spoken for.

And as he watched her reach out and pull Hope back to her side with effortless grace, while simultaneously removing a champagne flute from her sister's grasp, he was fiercely glad of the fact.

Everyone knew she was spoken for.

Everyone knew she was his.

At least, outwardly.

Jonathan's sudden laugh sounded in Christian's ear.

"Forget the banns," his friend grinned, "I wonder if you'll last the night."

Christian only took the time to bid his friend a quick goodbye, nodding to the man's beautiful wife as she arrived by his side, then hurried toward Elodie.

Tonight, he'd get time alone with her if it killed him.

It was time they had an honest conversation. One that would tell Christian if he could make Elodie happy. Or if he'd ruined her life.

ELODIE'S GAZE RAKED the glamorous ballroom, uncomfortably aware of the attention she was garnering.

It had been this way almost since her arrival in Town.

And it would only get worse as the city filled up.

Christian was one of its most eligible bachelors, so naturally, everyone was curious about the lady who'd taken him off the market.

She couldn't help but feel like a lot of them found her wanting.

The events she'd been attending this week were, after all, quite different to the ones she usually received invitations to.

Just this morning they'd received vouchers to Almack's. Mama had almost had to fetch her smelling salts.

It seemed the Brentford connection had dragged the Templeworth family a few rungs up the social ladder.

And whilst Mama was in raptures about that, and Hope was thrilled to have access to new prey, more often than not, Elodie just wanted the ground to swallow her.

She was constantly thinking that they must be wondering what Christian saw in her.

Though she had to admit, nobody had been outwardly cruel. And the men she came into contact with definitely didn't seem to wonder at Christian's choice. Not if their lascivious glances and blatant flirtatious comments were anything to go by.

She'd barely gotten a chance to speak properly to Christian.

When he wasn't being commandeered by his many, many London acquaintances, Mama was dragging her around Bond Street, insisting that she make her wardrobe fit for a viscountess.

The fact that they weren't yet married didn't seem to faze her mother in the slightest.

And when he came to call, their drawing room was so crowded that sometimes she didn't even get to greet him properly.

And she missed him.

It was a physical ache.

She wanted his arms around her, his lips pressed to her own.

She wanted him to bring her to the heights of pleasure that she'd only known in his arms.

Even the memory of his touch set Elodie's heart fluttering, and she wondered if the heat she felt inside showed on her skin.

"Thank the heavens! Lord Brentford is here," Hope declared. "Now, I might actually get to have a little fun while he distracts you. Bye, Elle!"

Elodie couldn't even warn her younger sister against impropriety, for all of her attention was now focused on the viscount prowling toward her.

Lord, but he was beautiful.

His clothing was all black, relieved only by the pristine white of his shirt and cravat. And as she watched him, she couldn't help but remember what was under the fine material fitting snugly to his body.

"Elodie."

He came to a stop in front of her, and though he'd only said her name, there was a world of feeling in it.

He quickly greeted her mother, who fawned and simpered before she spotted a baroness who was vaguely known to their family, and then she was gone, forgetting all about her daughters in the quest for social climbing.

Papa hadn't bothered accompanying them this evening.

As soon as her mother was out of earshot, Elodie let out a sigh of relief.

She'd missed him so much.

In such a short space of time, he'd come to mean so much to her.

But that guilt was still there. Ever-present and growing by the day.

She looked up at him now, trying to work out if he resented

her.

"You look beautiful," he said softly.

"So do you," she said with unthinking honesty, earning herself one of his heart-stopping grins. "Ah—is Mr. Harrison joining us? I confess we haven't seen or heard from him since, well, since that day."

She'd meant to ask about poor Philip all week, but truthfully, he hadn't been on her mind.

Her eyes widened as they took in the sudden icy fury on Christian's face.

"He's gone back to Halton," he said in clipped tones that hinted at a tight rein on his emotions. "He won't be back, and he won't be welcome around us."

"G-goodness," she said breathlessly, "what on earth did he do to you?"

He studied her face before finally sighing.

"I wasn't sure whether to tell you because frankly, I don't think it matters anymore, but—Philip is the one who spread the exaggerated tale of our incident at the Assembly Rooms in Halton."

Elodie's whole body froze in shock.

"Philip?" she repeated, aghast. "But-but *why*?"

"He thought to force me from the village and tarnish your reputation so much that you'd have no choice but to accept him."

Christian was watching her now with worry stamped across his face. And as his words sank in, so, too, did the reality of them.

Christian's own cousin, a cousin to whom he'd given no end of help, had caused all of this. Had forced him to offer for her.

Her mind was a riot of confused thoughts and emotions. But before she could voice any of them, he reached out and lifted her chin, forcing her to meet his gaze. "Thankfully, he didn't account for that spine of steel you have, my dear. Or that fire in your veins. He never would have thought you'd take control of your life the way you did."

He was being so kind. Was it possible that he didn't mind?

He studied her face closely again with that brooding intensity before his face cleared.

"I do believe these are the most words we've managed to speak to each other all week," he answered before grasping her hand and bringing it to his lips.

He watched her as he placed a soft kiss upon her glove, and Elodie could barely suppress a whimper of need.

What she was feeling must have shown in her expression, for his smile grew positively wolfish as he straightened back up.

"Let's go for a walk," he said, his voice suddenly gruff.

"Won't people expect us to dance?" she asked, though in truth, she could think of nothing better than being alone with him, away from the prying eyes of the ton.

"I don't give a damn what people expect," he answered before taking her hand and pulling her toward the French doors at the back of the ballroom.

Elodie could see a sort of veranda beyond the doors, lit with torches that led into a garden.

More than one person called a greeting or turned to wave, but Christian ignored them all, forcing Elodie to return their greetings with nothing more than a smile or a nod.

They'd just reached the back of the room when she caught the eye of an astonishingly handsome gentleman with a beautiful brunette on his arm.

The man was grinning knowingly in their direction, and he raised his glass in a sort of salute to Christian as he swept her outside into the cool night air.

"I-I think your friend was trying to get your attention," Elodie told him a little breathlessly.

"I don't care," he answered, still in that same gravelly tone.

Elodie began to wonder if something was wrong, he seemed so serious. So intense.

But as soon as they were down the steps of the veranda and into the darkened gardens, he spun to face her.

The torches along the path set flickering light across his face, making him all shadow and angles. Even still, his eyes glowed brightly in the moonlight.

Wordlessly, he pulled her from the path until her slippers sank into the mercifully dry grass that bordered it.

"Christian. What is it?" she whispered.

"I missed you, love," he answered, and her heart melted instantly.

If he'd missed her, surely he didn't regret their arrangement?

Before she could build up the courage to ask him, however, his hand reached out to grab the back of her neck and pull her mouth to his in a blazing kiss.

# Chapter Thirty-Two

ELODIE'S RESPONSE TO his kiss was immediate and explosive. Elodie's hands tangled in his dark hair. She could do nothing but hold on. She was captive to the feelings he evoked in her, a puppet, whilst he masterfully pulled her strings.

"Elodie?"

They broke apart at the sound of Hope's voice from the veranda.

Elodie made to move into Hope's line of sight, but Christian stopped her with a hand on her arm as he brought a finger to his lips, indicating that she should stay silent.

"Elle?"

After a moment, they heard her sister huff before sweeping back inside.

But the interruption had cooled Elodie's ardor slightly, and she was able to look at Christian's face with equilibrium.

Only very slightly, she thought with a shiver as he stood grinning down at her.

"What I wouldn't give to be traveling around the inns of England alone with you again," he said wryly.

Elodie couldn't keep her smile from her face in response.

He most certainly didn't seem upset by their engagement.

And he wasn't acting like a man who'd been backed into a corner with no way out.

He reached out and stroked a finger along one of her cheeks, his eyes filled with a tenderness that made her heart skip a beat.

Finally, he sighed in defeat.

"Come," he said. "We'd better dance, or someone else will be out here looking for you."

His jovial mood was contagious, and Elodie eyed him with faux severity.

"I shall have to check if your name is on my dance card, Lord Brentford," she said. "It wouldn't do to allow you to take liberties."

Christian's gaze became positively predatory as he reached up and ran a finger along the neckline of her gown.

"Trust me, love," he said, his voice low and rumbling, "dancing is not the liberty I want to be taking with you."

Elodie's legs began to shake in response to his touch, his voice, the scent of sandalwood that surrounded her now that he stood so close.

"But if dancing is the closest I'm going to get for now, then we'll dance."

"Well," she heard how shaky her voice was, and judging from his smug smile, he did, too, "I am not engaged for the next, we've already missed the first."

"You are not engaged with anyone but me for all of them," he growled proprietorially.

Elodie had no interest in spending time with anyone else, but she wouldn't give in too easily, either.

"I won't wish to be rude," she teased. "And we don't want to set tongues wagging with you looking like a jealous suitor."

"I don't give a damn about being rude," he answered. "And I *am* a jealous *fiancé*, not suitor."

Her heart thrilled at his use of the word.

"If I only get to see you at these interminable things, then I'm keeping you at my side for the entirety of them."

She gave in then because how could she not when he was so very wonderful?

"Very well," she said happily, earning herself another heart-stopping kiss.

She placed her arm in his own, and they made their way back toward the house.

Just before they entered the ballroom, Christian drew her to a halt.

"Elodie," he said softly, seriously. "Are you happy?"

It was the closest they'd come to any real sort of conversation since their forced betrothal. And it wasn't nearly enough. They needed to talk properly about so many things.

But in that moment, she chose to be honest. They could discuss it all another time.

"I couldn't be happier," she answered truthfully, and she knew that she was giving herself away, but she couldn't bring herself to care.

Christian's eyes filled with tenderness and what looked like relief before he placed a swift kiss upon her forehead.

"I'm glad," he said before sweeping her inside to the other dancers.

An uneasy thought sounded in the back of Elodie's mind as they took their place in front of all the curious eyes watching her.

He hadn't said that he was happy, too.

⇒⟫⟪⇐

CHRISTIAN WAS SURPRISED to find he was actually enjoying one of these ridiculous events. And it was all down to Elodie.

He didn't think he'd ever felt such pure, prideful joy as when she'd said she couldn't be happier.

They had a lot of talking to do, he knew.

This wasn't what either of them had planned for. But every second of every day, Christian grew closer to being deliriously happy that this was how things had turned out.

Perhaps it was time to tell his future wife that.

The orchestra plucked the beginning strings of the supper

waltz, and he pulled her into his arms, knowing full well he was holding her closer than he should but not caring a jot.

Let the whole of London see how much he desired his bride.

How could he not, when she was the most beautiful thing in the world to him?

True to his word, Christian had kept her glued to his side all evening.

And it wasn't just because he wanted to tear the eyes out of every man who shot her an admiring gaze.

It was because he was happier with her than without her.

She was bright and witty, with a wicked sense of humor.

And when he distracted her enough from watching over her sister, she relaxed and had fun, which was exactly what he wanted.

He introduced her to Jonathan and Gabrielle, and Jonathan's sister Anna and her husband Captain Townsend, who had lately arrived in Town.

And as they all laughed and chatted and extended invitations to dine together, Christian thought his chest would burst with the pride he felt at having Elodie by his side. His friends were as charmed by her as he had been.

His mother and sisters, who would arrive in time for the wedding, would adore her, he was sure.

Yes, quite by accident, his life was turning out to be rather wonderful.

The music came to an end as they were standing at the edge of the ballroom, surrounded by people. And it wasn't the right time, but suddenly, he couldn't help himself.

"Elodie," he whispered softly. "I—"

"Christian, darling. So it's true. You are back."

Christian froze.

Damn it.

Cressida.

He'd meant to call on her to end their arrangement, but well, truth be told, he'd been so occupied with Elodie that he hadn't remembered to.

He watched Elodie's frown of confusion, noticed the whispers all around them.

His affair with Cressida hadn't exactly been a secret, after all. It was common knowledge among the *ton*.

Everyone knew.

Everyone except Elodie.

Christian swiftly drew his features into a mask of politeness.

He would smooth this over as best he could to avoid embarrassing them all, then he'd get Elodie the hell out of here.

"Lady Cressida." He turned with a friendly but distant smile to bow at the redhead who was eyeing him curiously, a hard glint in her eyes. "We are not long arrived in Town."

The glint hardened as Cressida's smile slipped into a grimace. "We?"

Christian resisted the urge to pull at his cravat.

"Uh…yes." This was awkward as hell. "May I introduce my fiancée, Miss Elodie Templeworth? My dear, Lady Cressida Fenning."

Elodie's eyes flickered between Christian and Cressida, and he could see the questions lurking in their depths.

But being the impeccably bred lady she was, she curtsied prettily to the older woman, her face open and free of artifice.

Unfortunately, the same couldn't be said for Cressida.

Her smile put Christian in mind of a venomous snake about to strike.

"How do you do, Miss Elodie?" she simpered. "This must be quite the step up for your family, nabbing a viscount."

Christian felt a dart of anger at Cressida's rudeness, and Elodie's Flinched.

He didn't know what the hell Cressida was playing at.

He owed her a conversation, Christian knew. Perhaps even a bauble to mark the end of their time together.

But that was between them. Surely she knew that Elodie was naïve in their ways. That a rude remark might roll off the back of a jaded lady who'd been around the game long enough, but not off the back of someone as artless as Elodie.

"Cressida…" His warning was interrupted by the arrival of Hope Templeworth, who glided over, looking confident and radiant in pink satin.

"Elodie, dearest. I've been searching all over for you."

She smiled at her sister, her eyes, similar in color, seeming to convey some secret message. Christian watching Elodie as closely as he was didn't notice any change in her expression, but there must have been something, for Hope's eyes hardened before they turned to face Cressida expectantly.

"Lady Cressida, Miss Hope Templeworth," Christian said stiffly, uncomfortable with the undertones swimming around them.

A quick glance showed even more avid spectators, and he had to bite down a black oath.

"How do you do?" Hope dropped into a tiny curtsy, and Christian had to hold back a smile. He didn't know how the girl did it, but she'd managed to put a world of dislike into a pleasant question.

Cressida, for her own part, merely nodded her head regally.

"I was just complimenting your sister on her engagement to our Christian, here," she said, her smile not reaching her eyes.

"How kind," Hope's voice dripped with insincere sweetness. "Yes, we are all well pleased that Elodie has found happiness with *her* Christian."

A direct hit.

Cressida's eyes tightened at the none-too-subtle challenge.

And he felt a sudden wave of affection for the incorrigible Hope.

Elodie might spend her time looking after her sisters, but they looked after her, too. Fiercely, it seemed.

"Elle, could you accompany me to the retiring room? I think a hem has come down."

"O-of course," Elodie smiled weakly at her sister. "It was a pleasure to meet you, Lady Cressida," she said, her manners still impeccable in the face of Cressida's rudeness.

Cressida didn't even bother to answer, which set Christian's teeth further on edge.

Scowling, Hope took hold of Elodie and dragged her away, leaving Christian fighting the urge to run after her.

"What a meek little mouse you've caught yourself, darling," Cressida laughed.

Christian whipped his head back around to her.

"Watch yourself, Cressida," he bit, his temper flaring. "She doesn't deserve your spite."

Cressida's eyes widened slightly.

Christian had never snapped at her. He'd never cared enough about anything they discussed to snap, truth be told.

"Why, darling. If I didn't know better, I'd say you cared for the chit."

Christian pinched the bridge of his nose, wanting nothing more than to go to Elodie.

But he owed Cressida more than leaving her alone in the middle of a public ball.

"I meant to call on you," he said, his tone conciliatory. "I've just been busy."

"So it would seem," she quipped lightly, but there was an edge to it. "I imagine we will need to be more discreet for a while. But we can manage that."

There would be no managing anything, but now was not the time to tell her that.

"I'll call on you tomorrow," he said quietly.

She smiled a feline smile that he had surely found attractive in the past, but now it left him cold.

"Till tomorrow then, *mon cher*."

# Chapter Thirty-Three

CHRISTIAN WOULD RATHER walk over hot coals than have this conversation, but despite Cressida's behavior at last night's ball, he owed her a proper ending to their arrangement.

And after he left here, he was going straight to Elodie to tell her he loved her.

Because—he'd finally admitted to himself in the small hours of another sleepless night craving her—he did love her. Completely and absolutely.

He would have admitted it sooner, to her and to himself, if he'd properly recognized the emotion. But having never felt it before, he'd been blinded. By his fear of commitment, by his uncertainty about her own feelings, by his adamance that he'd wait as long as possible to marry and settle down.

Now, however, nothing gave him more joy than the idea of having Elodie all to himself, secreted away on one of his estates.

Or maybe he'd take her to one of the far-flung, exotic places in which he had his business interests.

He could just imagine her now, those eyes wide as they took in the sights.

Christian dragged his mind from thoughts of Elodie's skin, bare and sun-kissed, lest he embarrass himself in public. Last night's kiss had done nothing to assuage this yearning, constant need for her. Nothing except having her would. Even then, he didn't think it would ever go away.

The door to Cressida's townhouse opened, and the footman, immediately recognizing Christian, let him in.

The butler greeted him, too, as a familiar face, and Christian tried to ignore his discomfort at that fact while they made their way to Cressida's drawing room.

"Darling, come in."

Cressida jumped from the chaise she'd been occupying as soon as she saw Christian in the doorway.

Her gown was a deep purple, the neckline scandalously low, and she wore her long red hair loosely flowing down her back.

She was dressed for seduction. A reunion. And Christian couldn't wait to get the hell out of there.

"Branson, a bottle of the viscount's brandy, if you please," Cressida called to the butler.

"Ah, that won't be necessary, thank you, Branson," Christian interrupted. "I'm afraid I cannot stay long."

The butler didn't react save to bow and close the door behind him, but Christian knew the man must be wondering at his behavior.

He'd never called her for a social visit, and he had always stayed long.

"Well, I knew you'd miss me but not even to take the time for a drink? I don't know whether to be flattered or insulted," Cressida laughed, sauntering toward him.

Without warning, she reached up and pressed her mouth to his.

Christian immediately set her away from him.

"Cressida," he warned. "I'm here to talk and *only* talk."

"Talk? That's a first," she said. When he didn't respond, she shrugged, then turned and took a seat on the chaise again.

"Come then. Talk."

Christian heaved a sigh.

"I have always enjoyed your company, Cressida," he began. "And I have enjoyed our time together in the past. But as you know, I am to be married, and so I've come to say goodbye."

His statement was met with calculated silence before she burst into laughter, the sound grating on his nerves.

"Oh, my word. What has that little mouse done to my Christian? You cannot honestly expect me to believe that you're ending our relationship because of the chit at the ball?"

Christian's mood darkened.

How had he never seen how truly vicious Cressida could be? Perhaps because she'd never had cause to be. Not in front of him in any case.

"Elodie is to be my wife," he said firmly. "Do not disrespect her in my hearing again."

Cressida shot to her feet.

"Disrespect *her*," she hissed. "And what of me? You leave for the Americas for almost two years, then you come back here with some country nobody for a bride? How dare you treat me in such a fashion?"

Christian could only stare in shock at the angry woman before him.

He'd made her no promises. Not before he'd left on his travels, never.

And she'd never expected them from him either.

"I was very clear about what this arrangement was to me, Cressida," he said as evenly as he could. "I'm sorry if you're upset, but we both went into this with our eyes open."

Her face twisted with rage, making her almost ugly.

"And you'll throw me over for a naïve little girl with no idea how to please you?"

Christian would have lashed out, but he merely smiled, shaking his head.

"You have no idea what you're talking about," he said. "Nobody has ever brought me more happiness than Elodie."

Cressida flinched as though he'd slapped her, and Christian began to wonder if her feelings for him ran deeper than he'd ever imagined.

"I have no desire to cause you pain, Cressida." He tried to

bring their conversation back to a place of civility if not friendliness. "You were good to me, and I hope that I was good to you. But it's over now."

She shook her head. "No," she said furiously. "No, you cannot just end it like this. You'll come crawling back when your cold little innocent can't give you what you need. I know you Christian. I know what you need, and I can give it to you."

Once again, she threw her arms around him, and once again, Christian had to push her away, gently but firmly.

"She is everything I need, the only thing I want. I love her, Cressida," he stated firmly, his temper fraying with every insult she flung at him about Elodie. "She is pure and good and a breath of fresh air in this glittering cesspit we're all forced to endure."

He hadn't wanted to say those words for the first time to anyone but Elodie. But if that's what it took to get the other woman to accept how things were, then so be it.

Cressida merely stared at him, wide-eyed, her breathing labored. "You mean she's a naïve little fool. They'll eat her alive."

Reaching into his pocket, Christian pulled out the box he'd brought with him. He'd had enough of this conversation, and he didn't want to say something he'd regret. He'd never mistreated a woman before. He didn't want to be cruel now.

"Here."

He tossed the box onto the cushions of a chair.

"Something to thank you for being so understanding," he said sarcastically before turning and walking out.

The earrings had perhaps been a bad idea. But he'd wanted to assuage some of the guilt he felt, and when he'd spotted them in the jewelers, he'd bought them on a whim.

He'd been in there picking up a gift for Elodie. A necklace with the most unusual heart-shaped diamond at its center.

She would, of course, have access to all of the Brentford jewels, and would wear the Brentford diamond when they married, but Christian had wanted her to have something just from him, just for her.

Hoping that would be the end of it, Christian took his leave.

But Cressida, it seemed, was not above making a scene.

She hurried out of the door after him.

"Christian," she called.

He turned to face her, and she threw herself at him, grabbing his lapels in a vicelike grip.

"Don't do something you'll regret, Cressida," he warned her, quietly praying that nobody with a loose tongue would see this little display as he put his hands on her own to remove them from his body. "You are a beautiful woman with a lot to offer. You'll find someone who can care about you the way you want. Don't make yourself ridiculous on my behalf. Nothing you do will ever change my feelings for Elodie."

She looked at him, her eyes stricken, and he hated that he'd been so blind as to the depths of her feelings. But what he said was true. He'd never love anyone but Elodie until the day he died.

Cressida turned and swept back inside, closing the door firmly behind her.

Christian heaved a sigh and felt as though a weight had been lifted from his shoulders as he stood on the steps of Cressida's townhouse gazing up at the morning sun.

It was too early to call on Elodie, he knew.

But they were to attend another blasted ball this evening, so if he didn't see her this afternoon, he'd at least see her there.

Smiling to himself, he made his way toward his club to while away the time until he could see Elodie again.

ELODIE HAD FELT sick all morning as she remembered the current of tension between Christian and the beautiful redhead the previous evening.

Hope had been ready to scratch the other lady's eyes out, but

Elodie hadn't been angry at the woman's rudeness, just desperately sad.

It was obvious that there had been something between Christian and Lady Cressida.

Maybe even an agreement.

Did he love the other woman?

Had Elodie ruined his chances of being with the woman he loved?

She sat in the library miserable and afraid.

Christian had offered for her because he'd had no choice. Because he was good and moral and decent.

He'd asked her if she was happy. But he had never said that *he* was.

And he'd never intended their lovemaking to be anything other than temporary.

*I won't tell if you don't.*

She had thought he was keeping it a secret in deference to her reputation.

But was it because he was in love with another woman?

"You're being ridiculous."

Elodie looked up as Hope floated into the room resplendent in lemon silk.

"I didn't say anything," Elodie countered, affronted by the insult.

"Your face is saying enough," Cheska plopped herself onto the arm of Elodie's seat, her skirts floating around them both. "Hope told me about that viper at the ball last night. You mustn't pay her any mind, Elle. Bitter old hag."

Elodie was touched by her sister's defense of her.

"She was neither old nor a hag," she said miserably. "She was stunning, actually."

She looked to Hope for confirmation.

"She was pretty," Hope conceded. "You are prettier," she finished stoutly.

"What does it matter?" asked Elodie. "Clearly, there was

something going on that I wasn't privy to. And…" She swallowed a lump in her throat. "And Lord Brentford has never claimed to love me or even care about me."

"Elodie…"

Francesca reached for Elodie's hand, but she jumped up from her seat, too agitated to sit there being comforted.

"I'm not so naïve as to be unaware of how these *ton* marriages work," she said, trying and failing to sound sophisticated and unbothered. "Lord Brentford would hardly be the first gentleman to marry one woman while carrying on with another. He was forced into this. It wasn't his fault. He's doing right by me, but that doesn't mean he can just switch off his feelings for another woman. Or that he should have to."

"Are you mad?" Hope jumped to her feet. "Elodie, I see how he is with you. We all do. And last night, the way he watched you, there's no way he's in love with another woman."

"And what is this self-sacrificing nonsense in any case?" Francesca added. "It wasn't your fault, either. It was the stupid pig farmer."

Elodie had filled her sisters in on Philip's behavior, and they'd all been in high dudgeon with the man ever since. She felt sorry for him, despite the problems he'd caused, because when Hope, Cheska, and even Sophia returned to Halton, he'd have no peace.

"Yes, but—"

"But nothing. You were cornered into this marriage as much as the viscount."

"Well, it's different for me," she said, pulling agitatedly at the sprigged muslin of her gown.

"Why is it different?" Hope asked shrewdly.

Elodie huffed out a breath of defeat. "Because," she mumbled. "I love him."

She expected her sisters to mock her mercilessly, but when she looked up, they were merely smiling at her.

"Don't you think it's possible that he loves you, too? Even a little bit?" Hope asked.

And despite herself, Elodie felt a flickering of belief in her belly. He certainly acted as though he cared for her.

She was about to answer when Sophia came bursting into the room, pulling at the riding habit Mama had insisted she don if she were going to ride in public in London.

"Elodie," Sophia gasped, her hair flying about her face, two bright spots of color on her cheeks. "You won't believe what I've just seen."

"What?" Elodie was alarmed by the fearsome glint in Sophia's eyes.

"I've just seen Lord Brentford," she bit out, "wrapped around another lady on the steps of a house that is not his."

The quiet after Sophia's statement was horrible.

"What did she look like?" Elodie asked, but she already knew.

"I didn't get a good look at her face," Sophia said, her voice laced with anger. "But she had the most striking mop of red hair."

# Chapter Thirty-Four

"**Y**OU SHOULD HAVE spoken to him. Hiding won't do you any good."

Elodie tried to tune out Francesca's scolding as they traipsed along the Serpentine.

"You should let him in so you could stomp on his foot," Sophia interjected.

"And you cannot avoid him forever," Hope added most unhelpfully. "Mama would rather die than let you miss tonight's ball. And he said he was going to see you there."

"I know," Elodie huffed. "I just-I just need some time to think about all of this."

"What is there to consider?" Cheska demanded. "You tell him in no uncertain terms to keep his deviant behavior out of the public eye. I cannot believe you're still willing to marry him."

"I don't have a choice," Elodie responded for what felt like the hundredth time.

"You *do* have a choice," Cheska responded. "You didn't let yourself be forced into a marriage with Philip blasted Harrison, so why should you let yourself be forced into a marriage with his awful cousin?"

Elodie didn't have the patience to deal with this conversation. Not when she was trying so hard to fight her heartbreak.

"I've explained this to you," she said. "To all of you. The whole of London knows of the engagement. The banns are being read. This isn't some country scandal that can blow over. It's my entire life and yours, too."

She drew to a stop and turned to face the three of them. So dear to her, but so annoying sometimes she could wring their elegant necks.

"And I know none of you care," she said before they could. "But *I* care. And I won't ruin your lives because I've made a mess of mine."

"Let's at least break into her house with mice or frogs or something."

Elodie laughed in spite of her dire situation at Sophia's recommendation.

"It's no more Lady Cressida's fault that she loves Christian than it is his for loving her. Or mine, for loving him," she added, confusing even herself with her convoluted reasoning.

"Miss Templeworth. What a pleasant surprise."

Elodie and her sisters froze in dismay as one, before they all turned to face the subject of their conversation.

She forced herself to curtsy, her hand flapping subtly instructing her sisters to do the same. Which they did. Grudgingly.

Lady Cressida looked down on them all from atop her barouche before signaling for her footman to help her descend.

"My, there is a veritable hoard of you, Miss Elodie."

Elodie gritted her teeth at the woman's disdainful tone as she made the proper introductions.

She dearly hoped the lady would be friendlier than she had been last night.

Whatever chance Elodie had had of keeping Hope on a leash, there was no telling what Francesca or even Sophia would do.

"Will you be attending the Huntsford ball tonight?" Lady Cressida asked, running an eye over Elodie's sprigged gown and lavender pelisse. The look in her eyes said she found Elodie wanting in the fashion department.

"I shall be, yes," she answered with equanimity.

"Oh, it must be terribly exciting for your family. Attending the ball of not only an earl and countess, but a prince and princess. Yet another feather in your cap. You really were clever in landing Brentford, weren't you?"

Elodie tried to calm herself by taking deep breaths, but it was no use. The fiery temper that Christian claimed to love so much was awakening with force.

Still, she could not allow this spiteful woman to goad her into acting in an unladylike manner. She wouldn't stoop that low.

"We are all very conscious of the honor of Princess Lydia's kind invitation," she said, albeit a little stiffly.

Princess Lydia and Prince Alexander had been the talk of the *ton* not long ago. Their story was terribly romantic.

Elodie felt a pang of envy when she thought of the stories of how Prince Alexander doted on his English wife.

Enough to leave his own country and settle here for good. Enough to choose the earldom he'd inherited over the life of a royal in Aldonia.

That was true love.

Something, it seemed, that she would never experience.

Could Christian truly love this venomous, spiteful creature in front of her?

Lady Cressida was very beautiful but very cold.

And Christian was so charming, so warm, so ready to laugh and smile.

But then, Elodie had to concede that if things were the other way around, she'd want to scratch the other woman's eyes out!

"Oh, I'm sure you are. The countess is notoriously generous with whom she invites into her home. But you'll come to learn all of these things when you become the viscountess. Christian and I were only discussing it this morning at my home."

Elodie drew a swift breath at the woman's words.

She'd known, of course, thanks to Sophia. But until that moment, she hadn't realized that she'd been hoping her little sister was somehow mistaken.

How unspeakably cruel of the other woman to speak about it

so openly, so victoriously to her face.

Elodie could hear her sisters shuffling behind her, preparing for a fight, no doubt.

But she kept her chin up, her eyes fixed on Lady Cressida's.

"Indeed?" was all the answer she gave.

The other woman's smirk made her look suddenly older, less attractive.

"You don't look surprised," she said now, raising an eyebrow. "Perhaps you aren't as naïve as he supposed you to be. Well, good for you. You will survive a lot easier if you accept how things are. How things have always been. Christian and I—well, perhaps it's best left unsaid."

The lance of pain Elodie felt almost had her doubling over, and she knew that she wouldn't be able to marry him. Despite the dishonor and grief she would bring to her mother and her sisters, she simply wouldn't be able to live that sort of life. Where he left her bed to go to another woman's. Where she was a chore, an inconvenience, while he lived in secret with his real choice.

It would kill her.

It was already killing her.

Lady Cressida reached up and rubbed a gloved finger against the dainty diamond in her ear.

"But don't worry, Miss Elodie," she smiled venomously. "The rewards for us both will outweigh any...discomfort...I am sure. Why, these little trinkets were from him just this morning. He will be generous to us both."

The language from her sisters would have been more at home at a shipping dock than in the middle of Hyde Park, but Elodie couldn't move to scold them.

The world tilted beneath her feet as she eyed the earrings.

He'd never bought her a gift, she thought hazily, as though that were in any way important in the face of what Lady Cressida was saying.

"You are very pale, dear," Lady Cressida sneered as a parting shot. "I recommend Mademoiselle Longchamp's rouge cream.

It's quite the thing to redden your cheeks."

"So is a slap to the face," Francesca said suddenly, moving to stand protectively in front of Elodie. "Shall I demonstrate it for you?"

If Elodie hadn't been so heartsore, she might have laughed at how Lady Cressida's face paled at Cheska's threat.

Sophia and Hope stepped forward, too, each taking one of Elodie's hands. And they all watched silently as Lady Cressida climbed back into her carriage and drove away.

⇉⟫⟪⇇

CHRISTIAN COULDN'T SHAKE the feeling that something was wrong.

When he'd called on Elodie that afternoon, she hadn't been at home, and now she still hadn't shown up at the Huntsford ball.

He knew with absolute certainty that Mrs. Templeworth would never miss a Society ball. Especially one hosted by a legitimate royal family.

Perhaps it was just his unpleasant meeting with Cressida that morning that had him on edge.

His gaze caught Cressida's from across the ballroom. She was already on the arm of another man, her dress an eye-watering pink with dampened skirts if he wasn't mistaken.

She was obviously out to get attention—and it had worked.

He would have moved on from looking at her if he hadn't caught the vicious smirk, and the feeling of dread increased tenfold.

"You can't even take your eyes off her for a moment then?"

Christian spun around at the sound of Hope Templeworth's voice. She was glaring at him, her brown eyes fierce.

"I beg your pardon?" he said by way of greeting. Then, deciding that he didn't particularly care what she'd meant, he looked over her shoulder. "Where is she?" he asked.

"Who might that be, Lord Brentford?"

He frowned in confusion at Hope's unfriendly tone. He'd never heard her sound anything other than *too* friendly, truth be told. Only when she'd spoken to Cressida.

Cressida with that smirk—

Christian's stomach knotted.

"Where is Elodie?" he asked as evenly as he could manage.

"She's at home," Hope answered sharply, making him feel like a naughty child. "She wasn't particularly in a good mood considering the chat she had today with your *friend* Lady Cressida."

*Damn it.*

He should have known Cressida wouldn't accept their parting ways. Not after the way she'd behaved.

"What exactly did they chat about?" he asked, grim-faced.

"I'm sure you can imagine. You are a man of the world after all."

He swore profusely, not particularly caring that Hope could hear him.

"Listen, I don't know what Elodie thinks is going on between Cressida and me but—"

"But what? You didn't give her a gift? You weren't wrapped in an embrace in front of her house this morning for all the world to see?"

Well, when she said it like that, it sounded awful.

But he could defend himself at least partly.

"She said we were wrapped in an embrace? That is—"

"Oh no, that particular anecdote came from Sophia, who saw you both. Along with half of London, I daresay. And now Elodie is at home miserable. Not because you've humiliated her and crushed her heart, but because she feels *guilty* that you've been forced to tie yourself to her when you clearly want another woman."

Christian flinched.

Hope's words were like a dagger to the heart.

And he knew they were true. Sweet, kind Elodie. She would blame herself for his perceived unhappiness because she didn't know she was the only source of joy in his life.

"But I'll tell you this, you swine," Hope stepped forward, hissing and damned if he didn't feel scared into taking a step back. "You will *never* find a wife half so good as Elodie," she said. "She is the most wonderful person I've ever known, and she deserves to be loved. Fiercely and wholly. And if you can't see that she is a diamond, a prize far better than the Lady Cressidas of the world, then you're a bigger dolt than even Cheska thinks you are."

Christian was momentarily distracted, just imagining what the intimidating blonde had to say about him.

But he didn't care.

He couldn't care about anything apart from the fact that Elodie was hurting. Because of him.

Without a word, he turned to go but was stopped by her hand on his arm.

She dragged him back around to face her.

"Where are you going?" she demanded.

"I'm going to see my fiancée," he said firmly.

"No, you are not," she countered while he stared down at her.

"Excuse me?"

"You're not going anywhere near my sister," she snapped. "You will leave her in peace to pa—"

She stopped suddenly and clamped a hand over her mouth.

Christian frowned at her in confusion.

What had she been about to say?

*To pa—*

Suddenly, he knew.

"To pack?" he demanded. "Don't tell me she's bloody well running away again."

"It's none of your business," Hope said, but her eyes had dulled, and he could see that she was upset she'd ruined the plan.

These damned scheming Templeworth girls. They should all be locked up in cages.

"I'm surprised you're not back there helping like last time," he quipped dryly.

She tossed her curls back, refusing to be cowed by him, and she reminded him so much of Elodie just then that his heart squeezed.

"I'm the decoy," she sniffed. "Mama would rather die than miss this event. So I'm keeping her distracted until—"

"Until what?" he gritted, his patience wearing thin.

Because he wasn't traveling anywhere. Which meant that she couldn't be stowing away in his carriage again.

And that meant that she was more than likely putting herself in danger.

And a sudden, icy fear gripped him.

Hope stared mutinously up at him, and he knew she'd refuse to answer him unless he gave her a reason to.

"Hope," he said, his voice tinged with the desperation he felt. "I don't know what Cressida said today, and I don't know what Sophia thinks she saw, but I promise you, I have not so much as glanced at another lady since I met your sister. She—she is everything to me. I love her."

He could only wait, hoping that Hope saw the truth in his eyes and believed it.

After what felt like eons of her studying him intently, she sighed and nodded.

"If you make me regret this, we'll skin you alive," she said quietly, and Christian gulped because he truly understood they'd do it, too. "And we're probably too late in any case," she warned.

"I won't be," he said firmly. "Just…help me."

"Fine," she sighed. "Come on."

"You're coming?" he asked, surprised. "I thought you were the decoy."

"Yes, well. Things have evidently changed."

"Won't your mother be furious with you?"

Her grin was positively wicked.

"So, what else is new?" she asked before she took his arm and dragged him toward the exit.

# Chapter Thirty-Five

"**T**HIS IS NOT going to work."

Elodie quickly quietened down as Cheska turned to scowl at her.

She was right, though she dared not say it again.

It had been sheer luck that had helped her escape Halton. But escaping London in the middle of the Season, this time without a convenient viscount who was traveling in the same direction as she? That had to be beyond even the skills of the Templeworth girls.

Her heart thudded painfully as it had been doing every time she thought of Christian.

Despite her sisters' protestations that Lady Cressida was likely just being vicious, Elodie knew the truth deep down.

All of the intimacies she'd shared with Christian, all the conversations they'd had, and the time alone together—there had been ample opportunity for him to care for her. Perhaps even fall in love with her, as she had with him.

Yet it had never happened.

Now she knew that was because his heart had already been taken.

She loved him far too much to resign him to a marriage without love.

So, she'd run.

"I'd just like to point out that Bath is a terrible idea," Sophia interjected as she fiddled around with Papa's coach, attaching the horses and doing goodness knew what else. Sophia's knowledge around all things horseflesh was a mystery.

"I can't think of anywhere else to go," Elodie explained.

Her aunt and uncle never left Bath, but she was hoping that her cousin would travel to London for at least part of the Season.

It would be easier to avoid one man's roaming hands than two.

"Ah, got it."

"Don't you think Papa will notice his carriage missing?" Elodie asked.

"Do you want to go or not?" Francesca spat impatiently. "Because you were the one who said you wanted to leave London tonight."

The reminder calmed Elodie's nerves as nothing else would have.

"Yes, I want to go," she said contritely.

"The newer carriage would have been better, of course," Sophia said as she ran a critical eye over the coach. "But we can't risk waiting until Hope returns with Mama."

"It's fine," Cheska said stoutly. "It's only to get her to the stagecoach in any case. Now, Elle, do you have everything you need?"

Elodie nodded silently.

"Come along then." Cheska chivvied her toward the carriage door.

Sophia was going to drive, and Cheska was going to act as the footman. Both had stolen livery from the stablehands, caring not a jot that they were committing theft.

"It's not theft if it's borrowing." Sophia had rolled her eyes when Elle had questioned where they'd gotten their disguises.

As Elodie climbed into the carriage and shut the door, she couldn't help but remember her flight from Halton only weeks ago.

And she missed Christian with an ache that took her breath

away.

What she wouldn't give to have him here beside her, kissing her, and bringing her body to life in that earth-shattering way of his.

The carriage trundled out of their stables, and Elodie reached over and pulled the curtain as instructed, plunging the inside into darkness.

This conveyance was neither as luxurious nor as comfortable as Christian's, but Elodie didn't mind very much.

There was a late-night coach leaving from an inn about an hour's travel from here. And she was sure the public coach would be a lot less comfortable than this, so she'd better get used to it.

She clutched her valise to her stomach, trying to quell the butterflies.

Mama would have her head, of that there was no doubt.

But at least Christian would be free to be with the woman he loved.

Hope, Cheska, and Sophia were all as supportive as they had been during her first runaway plot.

She didn't deserve them. She would never be able to repay them for their help and understanding.

She would miss them if Mama decided not to allow her to return home.

And that meant that she would have lost Christian *and* her sisters.

And just like that, the tears she'd managed to keep at bay since she'd first seen Christian with Lady Cressida burst forth, and she could do nothing to stop them.

The carriage trudged onward, painfully slow in the London traffic.

All around her, members of the quality were to-ing and fro-ing from one soiree to another.

And she envied them their simple lives filled with parties and balls and probably little else.

Doubtless, none of them had ever felt the need to run from

two marriage proposals in as many weeks.

Her head ached, and her throat was sore from the crying, but she could not stop the tears.

It was only when the door was thrown open that she even looked up from the floor.

Straight into the furious face of Christian.

CHRISTIAN HAD DIED a thousand deaths as his carriage had raced as quickly as humanly possible through the crowded streets of London.

She was mad. Insane. Fit for Bedlam.

And as he jumped from his own carriage that had caught up with and forced the Templeworth girls to stop right before they'd reached the inn they'd been fleeing to and ran to tear open the door of theirs, he honestly couldn't say whether he was going to shake some sense into her foolish, beautiful head, or kiss her.

"Christian!"

Her eyes were huge and wet from her tears, and as he looked into her stricken face, Christian felt weak with relief, even as his heart twisted painfully at the sight of her tears.

He'd never been fond of a woman crying. But the sight of Elodie weeping, knowing he'd caused it, gutted him.

But he couldn't focus on that now. Not when the fear he'd felt for her safety was still coursing through his veins.

"Do you have any idea how much danger you were putting yourself in?" he snapped, concern making his voice shake. "All of you," he turned to glare at her sisters who were standing between his carriage and theirs now.

As one, they crossed their arms mutinously and stared him down.

Good God, they'd be the death of him.

He knew now that his role as big brother was likely going to be far more stressful than he'd given any real thought to.

But first, he had to convince their stubborn, hot-headed, beautiful sister to marry him.

"I wasn't in danger," she snapped at him, and he could see by the flash in her eyes that his tone had angered her. "And it's none of your business in any case," she finished.

"None of my business?" he repeated with an icy calm that he sure as hell didn't feel. "None of my business that the woman I'm marrying is racing through the streets of London alone? Running away to who knows where? Putting herself in the path of people I don't even want to *think* about?"

She glared at him, her tears well and truly gone by now.

"Well, luckily for you, I am *not* the woman you're marrying, so it's of no consequence. Now, if you'll excuse us, we need to be at the inn in ten minutes."

"I... you..."

He was so angry, so scared that she meant it, that he was speechless.

He could only glare at her. Furious with her, furious with himself, furious with Cressida and the whole damned world.

And he had no idea what to do.

He looked behind him toward her sisters, who were whispering furiously amongst themselves. And he could only imagine what they were saying. Hope, at least, should be in his corner. But who knew with these girls?

By now, Mrs. Templeworth would surely notice that her daughter had disappeared. Which meant that he'd have to deal with that blasted woman's screeching when he brought them all back like a pack of renegade minxes.

His head throbbed again.

"Where is your father?" he asked without much hope that the useless man would be any help.

"Why?" she asked mutinously, clearly unwilling to give an inch.

"Because I can't help but wonder how you all managed to get

away with this," he gritted. "Again. Did he accompany your mother and sister to tonight's ball?"

A snort of derision sounded behind him, but he kept his eyes on Elodie. On the center of his whole world, though she didn't know it.

"My father rarely comes anywhere with us. He doesn't particularly enjoy our company."

"Then your father is an idiot. Anyone with a bit of sense would take every opportunity to enjoy your company."

"Oh, that was nicely done," he heard a whisper behind him. "Very romantic."

"Fiddlesticks. I saw him with that horrible woman."

"Yes, and like most gentlemen, he's probably fluent in poppycock."

Right. Hope hadn't brought them round then.

"I think I have some explaining to do," Christian said softly to Elodie.

"Yes, you do," came a voice from behind him.

Right. That was enough.

"Do *not* run away," he instructed Elodie fiercely before he turned his back on her and faced her three sentinels.

Reminding himself that he was glad they were as protective of their sister as she was of them, he tried to calm his temper.

"Ladies, your sister and I have some things to straighten out. I'm going to send you home with my driver."

The middle one, Francesca, raised a brow in blatant challenge.

"You can try," she said softly, all the more frightening than if she'd shouted.

"We're not leaving our sister with you," the little one piped up.

"Perhaps we should go back," Hope said. "Mama will be climbing the walls, and if he manages to convince Elle to forgive him, we're going to be the ones stuck living with it."

They were absolutely outrageous.

Christian had visions of his future, trying to keep an eye on them all during Seasons and parties. Surely Elodie could see that only the greatest love would induce a man into taking that on?

He tilted his head to the heavens to pray for divine intervention or at least the patience to get through this bizarre evening.

"Francesca."

They all turned their heads as Elodie's voice sounded just behind him.

"Go home," she said softly. "Thank you, all of you, for your help. But I think Lord Brentford and I need to talk before I go anywhere."

Christian's gut clenched.

She wouldn't look at him. She still planned on leaving. But at least she was willing to talk.

That had to count for something.

It was an opportunity, he told himself fiercely. One he wouldn't squander.

"Stevens," he called to the driver, who'd been watching proceedings with rapt fascination.

His footmen, he noticed grimly, had been watching the ladies.

"M'lord?"

"Can you drive this back to the Templeworth home in Mayfair? I assume one of the footmen can handle driving Miss Templeworth and me?"

"Yes, m'lord." The driver doffed his hat before sprightly climbing into the driver's seat of Elodie's carriage.

Wordlessly, he lifted her from the coach, loath to let her go when he felt her lithe body under his hands.

He watched carefully as the sisters bent their heads toward each other. He didn't trust them not to make a break for it.

But after a brief whispered conversation, the three younger Templeworths moved toward their carriage. Francesca passed him with not a word, her nose tilted in the air; Sophia went next, scowling before she climbed in after her sister. Finally, Hope stopped and gave him a quick, encouraging smile before she turned to wave at the dazed footmen.

And then, mercifully, they were alone.

And he felt inexplicably nervous all of a sudden.

"Shall we?" he asked.

She didn't answer him, but she let him hand her into his carriage.

And that, he supposed, was better than nothing.

# Chapter Thirty-Six

ELODIE'S HEAD WAS reeling from the last couple of hours. From the whole day really, since she'd had that awful encounter with Lady Cressida. She'd been so sure of herself when she'd decided to run. So sure that she'd never see Christian again. Yet here he was. Right in front of her. Close enough to touch.

But he was so very angry.

And so was she, in a way.

Why did he have to come here acting for all the world as though he cared about her?

She'd given him the perfect opportunity to let her go and forget about her.

It would look to the *ton* as though she had cried off. He was free to visit with and give jewelry to whomever he chose.

"Elodie, he said gently." "Please—don't ever, *ever* attempt to run away by yourself again. Please. My heart can't take it."

She watched his face for some sign that he was insincere. But he looked truly worried, his pallor and the tightness around his mouth leading her to believe that he was genuinely worried for her safety. But how could that be when he'd been visiting Lady Cressida and buying her earrings?

Elodie refused to let herself hope. Refused to let herself think that there was any chance that Christian truly cared for her.

She couldn't even blame him. Not really.

He'd tried to do right by her. And he couldn't help it if he didn't love her, just as she couldn't help the fact that she loved him beyond sanity.

"Why do you care?" she whispered, a wealth of pain in her voice. "I have given you every opportunity to forget me. You can just go. Be with Lady Cressida. Lavish her with gifts. I'm-I'm not your responsibility anymore."

Her speech was met with a deafening silence.

*I don't care,* she told herself fiercely. *I needed to get it out, and I did. He can go now and be happy, and I'll—well, I'll find a way to survive.*

Christian reached up and rapped on the ceiling of the carriage, bringing the conveyance to a stop.

After a moment, the head of his footman appeared inside.

"Take us to the inn up the road," he told the footman, who nodded his understanding, then disappeared again.

"Wh-what are you doing?" Elodie asked, her stomach plummeting.

This was what she'd wanted. For him to let her go. For him to live the life he wanted.

So, she shouldn't feel like her world was ending just because he'd decided to do as she'd intended.

They rode in silence until the carriage drew to a halt in the courtyard of the inn.

This was it, Elodie thought, trying desperately to remain calm. This was goodbye.

"Thank you, Lord Brentford," she said as calmly as she could. It didn't seem right to call him Christian now. "I sincerely wish you all the very best."

He didn't speak, didn't even return her farewell.

So, with nothing else for it, Elodie moved to exit the carriage.

She hadn't even touched the handle before Christian reached out and grabbed her, pulling her onto his lap.

"What are you—"

Before she could finish her outraged question, his lips descended on her own.

And Elodie was lost.

THERE WAS SO much for them to talk about.

So much they had to get straightened out.

Yet Christian could do nothing but hold Elodie against him and kiss her as though his life depended on it.

His life *did* depend on it.

Was she really so blind that she could not see the truth?

Did she really think that he could casually sit here and allow her to walk out of his life?

He felt the hesitation in her lips beneath his own, and it killed him.

Christian knew that he was moving dangerously fast. That there was so much they needed to fix. So much they needed to talk about.

But it was no use.

Common sense was no match for the love he felt for her. The roaring blaze of her desire that set him aflame with the first touch of her lips.

He felt the pins in her hair come undone, gloried in the silken locks falling in a waterfall of mahogany tresses against his hand.

Still, it wasn't enough.

Shifting her body, he maneuvered her so she straddled him, her core pressed against the hard ache of his lust.

He growled as she pressed herself wantonly against him.

Christian no longer felt in control of the raging conflagration consuming them both.

Lifting her with one arm, he laid her upon the cushioned bench before hovering over her. Wrenching his lips from hers, he moved his hands restlessly to undo the ribbons of her cloak, wanting nothing more than to feel her smooth, satiny skin under his own.

"Christian." Her breathy moans were his undoing.

"I need you, Elodie," he groaned. "I need all of you."

Pressing his lips to her own once more, he moved his hand under her skirts, past the stockings, until he felt the heated smoothness of her skin. His hand reached for the apex of her thighs, his fingers searching for that magic spot that would bring her pleasure beyond her imagination.

"Christian, I—"

A knock sounded against the door of the carriage, and Christian sprang back from Elodie as though he'd been burnt.

Her eyes fluttered as she sat up, her hair gloriously unbound, her cheeks flushed.

"We've arrived, my lord," the voice of one of his footmen sounded from outside. "We're at the inn."

Christian cursed under his breath, dragging a hand through his hair.

He looked over at Elodie, her breathing as labored as his own.

"Wait here," he said when he could trust himself to speak. "Just-just don't go anywhere."

He studied her face, praying that she would do as he asked.

A noise sounded in the courtyard, hailing the arrival of the stagecoach.

He watched Elodie's face carefully as she looked out the window in the direction of the coach.

"Please, love," he said hoarsely.

She looked back at him and nodded once, but it was enough.

He leapt from the carriage and hurried inside the inn.

Hoping against hope that she wouldn't go back on her word, he set about procuring a room immediately.

Even if she wanted to leave, he had time before the stagecoach set off.

He could only pray that it would be enough.

# Chapter Thirty-Seven

ELODIE LOOKED AROUND the clean but sparsely furnished bedchamber, trying to keep her shaking to a minimum.

This was madness, she knew.

Right now, she should be ensconced in the stagecoach, waiting for it to take her to Bath.

But fool that she was, she couldn't resist him. Not when he'd kissed her as he had and reminded her of just why she loved him so intently.

This was—unorthodox, she knew.

By now, her sisters would have returned home, not with the news that she was halfway to Bath, but with the news that the viscount had stopped her coach and then commandeered her, while sending them back to Mayfair.

And in all honesty, she didn't know which scenario her mother would be more upset about.

The sound of the door opening had her whipping around to face Christian as he entered the room, closing the door behind him and, she noticed with a gulp, locking it.

"I'm sorry," he said suddenly. "For so many things, but for now, I'm sorry that I've dragged us to an inn. I just… I couldn't let you go. Not now, not without telling you—"

"Christian."

Elodie didn't want to have this conversation.

But it seemed that she had to.

With only minutes to go until the stagecoach left the court-yard, she didn't have much time to say what she needed to say.

"I want you to know," she said, her voice wobbling, her eyes firmly on the floor at his feet. "I appreciate how honorable you've been in offering me. I am grateful to you for—well, for so many things. Things I can't even put into words. But it is best that we part ways here and now. For-forever. I don't wish to be the person who stands in the way of your true love."

A knock sounded on the door before he could answer her, and he turned away, returning in only moments carrying a tray with a bottle of wine and two goblets.

"Just like our first night together, remember?" he asked, the oddest smile playing around his mouth.

His charm was like a lance to her heart.

"Christian—Lord Brentford, I have to go."

He sighed as he placed the tray on a table by the bed.

Then he looked straight at her, capturing her gaze.

"I have some things I need to say to you," he said. "And after I'm done, if you still want to go to Bath, I won't stop you. I'll even help you get there."

Elodie was so confused, so heartsore that she didn't have the energy to argue.

And so she simply nodded her consent, moving to sit in the sole armchair in the corner.

Christian stood before her before suddenly moving to crouch in front of her, reaching out to take her hands.

"Elodie," he said, strong emotions blazing in the pools of his eyes. "You said that you don't want to be the person who stands in the way of my true love. But that's exactly what you're doing. You're standing in the way of it."

And the pain Elodie had felt before was nothing compared to what she felt right now.

CHRISTIAN WATCHED THE riot of emotions across Elodie's face and promised himself that from this day forward, he would try everything in his power to prevent anything from hurting her ever again.

He'd meant what he'd said, too.

If what he had to offer her, his heart, his soul, his whole life wasn't what she wanted, then he would take her to Bath or anywhere else she wanted to go.

Knowing that she was happy, even if it wasn't with him, was enough. Loving her, even from afar, would be enough.

He had no idea how she'd become his everything, but she had, and nobody, nothing would ever take her place.

"And do you know how?" he continued.

"B-because you're in love with Lady Cressida, and you were forced to become betrothed to me," she whispered as tears ran unchecked down her face.

He let go of one of her hands to capture her tears with his thumb.

"I was never in love with Cressida, Elodie," he told her, hoping she could see the sincerity in his eyes. "I have never loved anyone." He took a deep breath, preparing to lay himself bare. "Not until you."

Her eyes widened, and her jaw dropped open, and even though he had to say his piece, he couldn't help the stirring of desire he felt at the movement.

"But-but you said I was standing in the way of your true love," she sniffled miserably.

"And so you are," he answered with a soft smile. "By running away, by taking yourself out of my life—you are ruining any chance I have of living a life filled with love. Because I love you. Only you. *Always* you. And if you go, you'll be taking my heart and any chance of happiness with you."

"Christian."

It might have been wishful thinking on his part, but he thought he heard longing in her tone.

"Sophia saw you with Lady Cressida, and that woman. She said—"

"What did she say?" he asked, trying to keep his temper in check.

If Cressida ruined any chance of happiness for him, he'd never forgive her.

"She said that you bought her those earrings and that, that you and she had an understanding that I was too naïve to understand."

Christian sighed, jumping to his feet and running a hand through his hair.

"Sophia didn't see what she thought she saw," he told her. "What she saw was me saying goodbye. I won't lie to you. Before I left England, Cressida and I had an arrangement. But that arrangement ended the second I laid eyes on you at that country dance." He smiled. "And I should have told her sooner, but by the time we'd come to London, I was so in love with you, I couldn't think of anything outside of you."

He began to pace, his words falling over each other, so desperate was he to get them out.

"When we saw her that night at the ball, I realized I needed to see her. To leave her under no illusion about us. About me and how I felt about you. She got…upset when I called on her. Tried to…well, it's no matter. But I promise you, there has been nothing between us since I met you. Since before then! And I'm so sorry that you were hurt, but I promise if you can forgive me, I will never hurt you again."

Elodie was shaking her head, and it put the fear of God into him.

"The earrings—"

"The earrings were a stupid, spur-of-the-moment purchase to say goodbye," he groaned. "If I'd known that she'd use them as a weapon against you, I never would have gotten them. I only bought the bloody things because I was in the shop buying you a gift."

"You-you were?"

She looked so innocent, so surprised that he should want to buy her something that his heart thudded painfully.

No matter what he said here tonight, he'd never deserve a woman as loving, as good, as kind as her.

"I was," he smiled, reaching into his pocket and pulling out the necklace.

"It's beautiful," she said as he crouched before her once more and held it out.

"An indestructible heart," he said softly. "Did you know that diamonds are one of the strongest materials in the world? That's why I got it. It's a representation of my love for you. My heart is yours forever. My love is yours forever. And nothing could ever destroy it."

"Do you really mean it?" she asked, sounding a little breathless. "Because I can't marry you if you are going to carry on an affair elsewhere, Christian. Perhaps that makes me naïve but—"

"It doesn't make you naïve, love," he interrupted fiercely. "It makes you pure and good. Too pure for the stupid games the *ton* plays. Better than I've ever been. But I want to be the best version of myself for you. And I love you so much. I want you so much that I could never want anyone else."

"So will you stay?" he asked. "Will you marry me? Will you give me the gift of true love?"

She stared at the heart still outstretched in his hand, and his own heart stopped while he awaited her answer.

Finally, she looked up at him and smiled, her face radiant, her eyes glowing.

"I will," she said through a fresh batch of tears. "I love you, Christian. So very much. I just wanted you to myself. All of you."

"Thank God," Christian whispered before standing and pulling her into his arms.

"You have me, love. All of me. Forever."

He kissed her until they were both breathless before lifting her from her feet and carrying her to the bed.

"We really shouldn't stay here," she said, though she wrapped her arms around his neck and pulled him against her.

"No, we shouldn't."

"My family will be wondering what happened," she gasped as he kissed her jaw, working his way down her neck and lower.

"I'm sure they will."

"My mother will be furious," she warned as he began to open the tiny buttons on the front of her dress. "And we'll never be able to explain this away. She'll want to know what we've been up to."

Christian stopped his task long enough to look into her eyes and smile.

"Well, love," he whispered. "I won't tell if you don't."

# Epilogue

"I'VE NEVER BEEN so glad to be at a country inn in my life."

Christian grinned at his wife as he closed the door behind them.

"Nor have I, love," he said, reaching up immediately to pull off his cravat.

It had perhaps been unconventional for them to have left their wedding breakfast early.

Even more unconventional that they'd immediately quit Town, not for a luxurious European honeymoon—at least not for another two weeks—but for an inn of little consequence on a road out of London.

He must remember to thank her scheming sisters, who'd played a blinder in getting them out of the ballroom of his townhouse without so much as a goodbye to any of their guests.

He raked his eyes over his viscountess, hardly daring to believe that she was finally his.

When he'd returned her to her family home that night weeks ago, he'd thought he'd never escape her mother's wailing.

Even her father had looked momentarily interested in his eldest daughter's fate.

But he'd soon smoothed things over by mentioning his mother's desire to meet with the family and offering up his coin to buy them all the finest gowns money could buy for the upcoming wedding.

It was vulgar, of course, for him to even make such an offer. But he'd known that Mrs. Templeworth would happily sacrifice any and all moral quandaries in the name of high fashion.

At least in Elodie's case, his money had been put to good use.

He watched her now as she removed diamond pins from her hair, watched mesmerized as it tumbled down her back.

She wore the heart he'd gifted her, and now she wore the Brentford diamond to match. Because she was his. Finally, irrevocably his.

Standing, she smiled coyly at him before turning her back and pulling her hair over one shoulder.

"Could you help with the buttons, darling?" she asked, her husky voice heating his blood to boiling point. "I can't reach them by myself."

Christian swallowed hard as he walked toward her.

The blue silk gown, chosen because it reminded her of his eyes, she'd said, was beautiful. There was no denying it. And he was sure that she'd want to treasure it forever.

"This is going to take all night," he groused as he eyed what seemed like hundreds of tiny, diamond-studded buttons down her back. "Can't I just rip it?"

"Patience is a virtue," she said piously, though her breath hitched as he leaned down to place a kiss upon the exposed skin of her neck.

"When have you ever known me to be virtuous?" he asked.

"Never," she answered. "But it would be a shame to ruin such a beautiful dress."

His jaw clenched against his acute disappointment.

But then she spoke again, reminding him exactly why he'd fallen in love with her.

"Christian?" she whispered as he set to work on the tiny, ridiculous buttons.

"Yes, love?"

He heard the smile in her voice though he couldn't see her face.

"I won't tell if you don't."

DAWN BROKE OUTSIDE the small window of the inn just as Christian thrust home, burying himself inside Elodie, bringing her to the heights of ecstasy for the third time that night.

The ache she'd felt when they'd first joined together that evening had long since passed as her husband showed her time and again just how skilled a lover he was.

And now he was all hers. Only hers. Forever.

Elodie felt the now-familiar stirring inside her and prepared for the explosion that she knew was to come.

And when it broke like a wave crashing over her, she stifled her cry of ecstasy against Christian's shoulder, holding on as he found his own release.

She floated back to earth, nestled in his arms.

Christian kissed her head, stroking a hand up and down her arm as she glided between waking and sleep.

"Elodie?" he whispered.

"Hmm?"

"Have I ever told you how glad I am that you tricked me into kidnapping you?"

She laughed sleepily.

"Not as glad as I am that you caused such a scandal," she answered before drifting into a deep sleep in the arms of her loving husband.

# About the Author

Nadine Millard is an international best-selling author hailing from Dublin, Ireland.

Having studied and then worked in law for a number of years, Nadine began to live her dream of writing when she had the first of her three children.

She released her debut novel in 2014 and has been writing ever since.

When she's not writing she can be found reading anything she can get her hands on, ferrying her three children to school and clubs, spoiling her cat, her dog, and snatching time with her long-suffering husband!

You can find out all about Nadine and her books at www.nadinemillard.com.